MIDNIGHT DANCE

A Seattle Sound Series Romantic Suspense Spin-off

by Alexa Padgett

Edited by Sarah Allan and Kathleen Payne
Proofread by Charity Chimni
Cover Design by Chris Philpot

ISBN: 978-1-945090-30-1

Also by Alexa Padgett

The Seattle Sound Series

Sweet Solace

Between Breaths

Hold You Close

Many Sounds of Silence

From the First

Striker's Waltz

When We Fell Down

A Moonlit Serenade

Moonshine Eyes

An Austin After Dark Book:

Deep in the Heart

Broken Rose of Texas

Austin By Morning

Rev. Cici Gurule Mystery Series:

A Pilgrimage to Death

A Heritage of Death

An Artifact of Death

A Revelation of Death

Identical Death

Standalone Mystery:

Facing the Past

Standalone Steamy Romance:

Trail of Secrets

The Echo Series:

The Spirit Seducer

The Magician's Ruins

The Curse of Kuskurza

Demons & Ultimatums

To my beta readers, Kate, Antje, Sandi, and Rachel, you are a keen eye and your feedback was invaluable. Thank you for your time, energy, and cheering for this novel. It means the world to me.

FOREWORD

I don't normally write a foreword, but I felt it necessary for this book. This novel came about because I've had requests for Colt's story for a while...as well as a strong itch to focus more on the suspenseful side of romance. This book allowed me to tackle both and I'm pleased with the result. I hope you will be, too.

I've described this as a "bridge" book to my author friends and my PR team because I wanted to introduce you to a new set of characters, starting with Nick Fowler. He's getting a full-length novel sometime soon (as soon as I can manage to write one worth reading!). But I struggled because the Seattle Sound Series, while gritty, isn't the same kind of gritty as Nick's world. Colt and his friends deal with addiction, adultery, abuse, mental illness, and sexual assault to varying degrees, but Nick... he's seen the worst the world has to offer, hell, he's lived it. So, addressing those concerns required me to thread the needle between the worlds *just* so.

I hope you feel I've done so. Of course, there are sexy-hot times in this book—Colt and Tawny are a steamy couple. But there are also elements (mostly from Nick) that push the boundaries of law enforcement and create a code of ethics that doesn't always mesh exactly with our culture's preconceived ideas.

That's what made this book so exciting to write. It fits into the Seattle Sound world, but…it's *more*.

At least I hope you find it so. And I hope you enjoy Colt's journey to finding Tawny, and eventually finding love.

Warmly,
Alexa

Chapter 1 | Colt | Saturday

Watching my younger brother stare into his new wife's eyes as they shared their first dance sucked massive donkey dick.

Don't get me wrong, I loved my brother, and Clay and Abbi were perfect for each other. *Perfect.* And I was a jealous sack of shit who couldn't shake the envy rippling across my skin and the soul-deep frustration that my baby brother found his bride before I managed to land mine.

Everything had been cool until Kara, my ex-girlfriend, walked into the reception venue, stopping at an archway covered with small red flowers and berries that, as my little sister Cassidy pointed out, matched Abbi's bridesmaids' dresses and bouquets.

The effect, especially against the wood-beamed ceilings and the gauzy white cloths that hung around the outer edge of the space, created an epic winter wonderland—a gorgeous backdrop to Clay and Abbi's perfect night.

The night that my now-ex, who I'd spent part of the last year trying to forget, was trying to ruin for them.

I was pissed off *and* shocked. For the record, that's hard to do when your father was an international rock star. Still, she showed serious audacity, showing up at my baby bro's wedding reception like that. No way in fuck was she invited. And where was the security my parents spent so much money on each month? Stopping breaches at important events was the *whole point* of having a private army.

Damn Kara for her audacity. At one point, I'd found that attractive. Not anymore. A while back, I'd thought Kara was the one. Apparently, she still managed to turn me inside out, even though I knew what a scummy person she was. This...*this* was why I'd sworn off women. Because I couldn't trust myself to make good emotional decisions where she was concerned.

As I watched Kara take in the beautiful room full of famous, powerful people with a greedy stare, the last of my hope to find someone who loved me for me—not for my dad's fame and money—shattered.

With these thoughts, I bee-lined over to Kara, my blood pressure escalating as a small smile bloomed across her lips. As if she expected me to fall in line with her plan to...I assumed...get back together.

No way. I wanted her out of here. Pronto.

The closer I walked, the more I noted the red of Kara's flattering dress. It made her tits look amazing and had been designed to emphasize her sensuality and delectable curves. Kara's dark hair fell in a long cascade down her back, the front swooping dramatically over her brow. She was dressed for seduction, not for celebration. Part of me was turned on. A larger part of me was pissed off that I was turned on. Kara was beautiful and smart, but she was also calculating, and clearly, those seduction tactics had worked before on me. So much so, she'd just door-crashed my brother's wedding.

Clearly, nothing with this woman was sacrosanct. And that shit didn't fly with me.

As I passed him, my father tossed me a look, eyebrows raised.

"You okay to handle her, Colt?" he asked.

"Yes."

"All right, then. Holler if you need any help."

As soon as I reached Kara, I gripped her upper arm and led her straight back out the way she'd come.

"What the hell do you think you're doing?" I growled.

I wasn't a growler. I was the thinker—a scientist, the logical, rational one in my family of artists. But, right now, I was lit up brighter than the sparklers we would use to send my brother off to start his happily-ever-after. The one this woman could ruin if I didn't get her out of there, stat.

"I wanted to talk to you," Kara said, fluttering her lashes. "To discuss our...future."

I paled, worried for a moment that she was pregnant. Wait. No, she'd definitely be showing a substantial bump if I'd gotten her pregnant.

And, if anything, she looked better than she had while we were together. I also knew she never mentioned a child or had a pregnant belly in these last months before I'd stopped checking her social media photos. That was when I'd been trying to understand how she could dump me for a man twice my age.

Awareness pumped through me as I remembered that greedy look she'd cast when she entered the room. I'd never been the prize she wanted. Power, prestige...that's what Kara craved.

I was simply a teaching assistant at Northwestern, working on my Ph.D. A nobody with a famous father. She'd latched onto me for my name—my pedigree—and when I failed to produce the desired results, she dropped me faster than a hot potato. How I'd been so hoodwinked, I couldn't say. But more with each passing second, I realized I'd dodged a bullet.

"So you thought it would be appropriate to crash my brother's wedding?" My voice turned more menacing.

The hurt I'd carried around all this time morphed into righteous anger. How *dare* she take something important to my family and trivialize it?

Kara blinked, her lips parting slightly as if she were finally beginning to understand I was pissed.

"Y-you wouldn't answer my calls. Or return my texts."

I straightened so I stood at my full height. I let go of her arm and stepped back, still blocking the entrance. No way she would get another look at my family, more gossip to share with her friends.

"There was a reason for that," I snapped. "I don't want to talk to you. Or look at you. Or ever see you again."

"Colt—"

"There isn't one thing you can say to me that will make me forgive your selfishness tonight," I said.

"I'm sorry for how I ended things. I-I want to get back with you. We were so good together." She tilted her chin and met my gaze with hers. "Let me prove how much I want us."

And I felt…nothing.

"I loved you," I mused as I studied her.

She shifted, no doubt thinking she'd won this round, expecting me to fall into her bed and beg her to spend my family's money. Yeah, that was a huge part of my appeal. Kara wanted my parents' wealth and prestige, which would never be mine. They expected me to work for what I had, and I did. That wasn't to say they didn't provide me with great perks, because they did, but I adhered to a budget and refused additional offers of financial assistance. I wanted to make my own way, wanted my parents to be proud of me. Once Kara realized that, she dumped my ass for some investment broker asshole. I hoped the sex was terrible.

"I still love you, Colt." She stepped closer; palm raised to lay on my chest. I shifted my weight and crossed my arms to block her attempt. No way would this woman touch me. She didn't have permission to breathe my air, let alone put her hands on me.

"Bullshit." My voice cut deep and hard, and she flinched. "You never loved me, which was why you dumped me—"

"I wanted to keep things casual. You were so intense, wanting to tie up our future. I was…" She licked her lower lip, no doubt shooting for seduction, but only managed to look nervous.

"I don't care what you were. Or what you are now. We"—I pointed between us—"are over. We have been since the moment you fucked the banker. It just took me longer to find out."

"Don't do this to us, Colt," she whispered, eyes filling with tears. "Don't throw our great love away."

From the corner of my eye, I caught bodies moving in our direction. Security. I grimaced. Their job had been to keep crashers like her, and all the press, out in the first place.

"You did that. *You.* Grow up and live with your choices."

"He left me."

I shrugged and stepped back as three security officers in suits swarmed around us.

"Sorry, Mr. Rippey. She told us she was your date. Had pictures of you together."

"She's my ex. And always will be. Make sure she doesn't get back in the venue or get anywhere near my family—any of them—again."

Their frowns deepened as they realized how much they'd fucked up. What had she offered them? A kiss? A blow job? Just a view of that tight, sexy body? I slid my hands into my pockets. Well, clearly, the males of our species weren't as clever as we wanted to believe if so many of us were blinded by female curves.

"Colt—" Kara pleaded.

"Don't ever—and I mean *ever*—contact me again." I turned on my heel to re-enter the venue.

But the doorway was blocked by my mother. She frowned, a slight crease between her brows. Her makeup was flawless and natural-looking, her wild hair, that I'd inherited, tied back in a complicated style that suited her elegant neck and pointed chin. Her dress was long and silky, flowing over her frame without being clingy or suggestive. My mother owned grace and dignity, creating an even starker contrast to Kara's blatant sexuality. Even the guards noticed, shifting again, no doubt realizing they'd thought with their dicks.

My heart rate escalated as I noted the fire in my mother's eyes.

"Lee?" Mom said. One of the security personnel peeled off, heading back toward my mother. "If she isn't gone in under a minute, I'm firing you."

My mother was sweet—one of the nicest people ever. But she wasn't happy, and she was making sure the staff understood the depth of her displeasure.

"And, Kara," my mother added, raising her voice. "If you don't abide by Colt's wishes, and if you decide to make trouble at my child's wedding or in any of their lives in the future, the entire city will find out what a diabolical bitch you are."

Kara gasped, her gaze shooting to mine. I stood, stone-faced, as the two remaining guards ushered her away. Lee brought up the rear as Kara looked back. My mother tugged me inside.

"I never liked her, Colt. I just want to point that out."

I smirked. "Diabolical bitch?"

Mom smoothed the front of her dress, her hands trembling. "She dumped you, then when the going got tough in her new relationship, thought she could slither back into your bed and good graces. Seemed like the term fit."

Ah, hell. My mom wasn't really talking about me. She was transferring her anger and resentment and other ugly emotions about my father's affairs onto Kara. No, it wasn't fair, but my mother couldn't do anything about those other women. Yeah, he'd had more than one sexcapade in his years of touring—that had come out when Clay broke up with Abbi, fearing he'd end up like our dad. I didn't know all the details, but I was glad Clay and Abbi patched up their relationship and that my father took ownership of his shitty decisions.

And it seemed that my mother had just taken out her need for revenge on Kara. While I wasn't sure her choice was healthy, at least I could understand her reasoning.

I pressed a kiss to my mom's cheek, hoping to relieve some of the tension sizzling off of her. "You were a badass."

She smiled but it didn't reach her eyes, and her face appeared pale. My father started toward us, but I shook my head, making sure he saw the warning in my expression. He nodded, his facial features pulling taut as he must have realized what set my mom off. Dad's infidelity was a painful undercurrent to my folks' relationship—one that seemed to be getting worse, not better.

Dad knew he'd fucked up, literally. My mother was brave enough to tell him so and then to forgive him, or at least try to. How she found that strength, I wasn't sure. And now that I witnessed her anger and continued pain, I wondered if she would ever be able to truly let Dad's affairs go. The possibility of my parents failing to reconcile and return to a loving marriage left me with a hollow, haunted feeling in the pit of my belly.

None of those thoughts should be going through my head on my brother's wedding day. I should be focused on Clay's love for Abbi, not the implosion of my love life and the continued fallout from my dad's bad decisions.

Even if those realities gave me yet another good reason to steer clear of romantic entanglements.

I pulled my mother to the edge of the dance floor and into my arms. "I need to dance with you, BAM."

"What's that?"

"BAM—Bad Ass Mom."

She smirked, some of her color returning. I glanced down at the violet dress she wore so well. My mother was a lovely woman. Her hair gleamed under the lights. I knew she dyed it, but she didn't have many grays to begin with. Her features were delicate without being fragile and her eyes held humor and secrets that would probably break me.

She let me take her fine-boned hand and lead her in a waltz.

Mom was hurting. Dad was, too. Maybe you got a shot at real love and maybe it fucked you over. I glanced at Abbi and Clay, hoping they had the lasting kind, the kind I wanted so badly I could taste the tang of envy on my tongue.

But I'd give up my own eternal happiness for my brother and my parents. In a heartbeat. Maybe less. So, it was time to stop being a jealous ass and start paying attention, start being a better brother and son.

By the end of the dance, both Mom and I were in better moods. My father appeared at Mom's side, his eyes questioning. I handed Mom off to him and he held her close to his chest like the treasure she was.

Good. At least they were enjoying the wedding. I looked around for my younger sister Cassidy, who was in an animated conversation with Abbi's thirteen-year-old stepbrother, Mason. They were the same height, but that wouldn't last long. Cassidy's dark hair hit her shoulders, such a difference from the fly-away blond locks of her youth and before her cancer treatments.

Clay and Abbi sat at the head table, grinning at something Abbi's mom, Dahlia, a beautiful woman with serene gray eyes and long reddish hair, and her stepfather, Asher Smith, said to them. Both Asher and Dahlia beamed as they looked at their daughter and son-in-law.

Clay and his bride sparkled brighter than a Times Square billboard. My parents joined them; their smiles effervescent.

As I watched, Clay raised their clasped hands and pressed a kiss to Abbi's knuckle, right above her wedding ring. She met his eyes, her smile warming. Her hair was tucked back in some intricate twist thing with curls touching her temples and the back of her neck. Abbi looked like the picture-perfect bride, but it was more to do with how she looked at Clay than what she was wearing.

I inhaled deeply, then exhaled. Getting rid of Kara once and for all felt good. Damn good. As did setting a course for my life. Like I was finally letting go of my past and ready to take steps toward my future.

I snagged a glass of champagne and lifted the flute, draining the liquid in two gulps. Not my first glass and it wouldn't be my last—I wanted to release the residual tension from my flare up with Kara. I'd already given my speech and planned to let loose. I wouldn't ponder how Clay managed to try to throw away love, and yet got it so right, while I utterly failed at relationships. I glanced at the open bar Asher Smith so generously provided. I lowered my glass and ambled over, winking at the pretty bartender who smiled back, flashing a dimple even as she plucked a clean glass and a bottle of champagne from the row lined up in front of her.

Up close, she was prettier. Desire pooled low in my belly.

Nope. Not acting on that, no matter how pretty she was. *Had I learned nothing from my altercation with my ex? From my parents' continued struggles?*

"Got any scotch back there?" I asked.

Her brows pinched but she nodded.

"Great," I said. "Fill 'er up."

"Um…"

I winked. "I'm the brother of the groom."

Her mouth twisted, her eyes cooling. "And you're in love with his bride?"

My jaw dropped, slack with shock. "What? Fuck, no."

She shrugged. "Wouldn't be the first time I had a jilted brother having a drink and sobbing out his woes at my station."

I was deeply offended she thought I'd ever do something so callous and unbearably stupid.

But I did yearn…no that wasn't a strong enough word. I *burned* for a woman to love with the same all-consuming passion and focus that Clay and Abbi shared.

"My ex showed up tonight," I said, my voice flat.

"That's uncool—unless you wanted her back." The bartender leaned forward on her station.

"Nope. I don't take back cheaters or liars."

A dimple flashed in her cheek. "Smart man."

"Allows me to avoid some emotional baggage. I hope."

"Will it?" she asked.

I stared down at the glass as the amber liquid began to glug into it. I didn't want the liquor. I didn't want anything to dull the way I was feeling now. Remembering how terrible I felt as my old love tried to reinstate herself in my life—that was my best line of defense.

One I needed to remember.

"Fuck if I know."

Chapter 2 | Colt | Saturday

I glanced back at the bartender, then at the wedding guests. The music throbbed through me. Two women tried to catch my eye. I downed a good portion of the scotch and set it on the counter, gesturing for another. Amber liquid splashed into the glass. The bartender leaned forward and slid a small piece of paper into my pocket.

"In case you're awake...and need a ride later."

I turned my attention back to the bartender. Her uniform of dark pants and blouse was prim. Her hair, though, was a wild cascade of large curls, and she'd done that cat-eye thing with her eyeliner, making her eyes stand out. They were pretty. A rich, dark brown I could drown in.

I liked them. I liked her.

And if I took her up on her offer for a ride, how would I look into my mother's eyes, knowing how she felt about one-night stands? How they'd shattered her trust and her confidence?

Did I want a meaningless fuck with a woman I had no intention of seeing again? How did that make me better than Kara?

She'd looked hot tonight, just as she'd intended. What pissed me off wasn't how good she looked—I'd been attracted to her from the start for that very reason. No, Kara weaponized her looks and body to get what she wanted, but I'd been too horny to notice before. Kara was still Kara, but something in me had changed.

I clasped the crystal tumbler, trying to drown out the rising noise of the crowd.

I needed to get out of this situation. I needed to understand why I hadn't seen Kara clearly while we were dating. Sure, I was angry with her, but a lot of that was self-directed. I'd brought her into my life—into my family's lives—because I must have been a shallow prick who thought more with his dick than with his brain. Clearly, I needed a break from everything.

Maybe I should visit the cabin at Lake Quinault. There, I could think more clearly about the request for an interview I'd received last week for a tenured position in the science department at the University of Wyoming.

"You know what? I've changed my mind," I said to the bartender.

I pulled out her number and dropped it into the glass. She didn't bat an eyelash, which surprised me.

Instead she smiled a little as she took the glass and emptied it behind her. "Wasn't my number," she said.

I raised an eyebrow.

"I wondered what kind of guy you were. Had me worried for a minute I'd misjudged you."

"What was it, then?" I mumbled. My vision was a bit fogged. How much had I had to drink? Too much.

"That was the number for a cab company."

"Why do some women use their bodies and looks to get what they want?" I asked.

The bartender shrugged. "No shame in using what you got.

This is a tough world."

"You're smart," I said.

"You're drunk," she shot back.

"A little."

She poured me a glass of water and shoved it into my hands. "Drink it. I'll get you another. Call someone to get you home."

"I have a room here. If I decide against that, I'll get a ride." I raised my hand at her wary look. "Promise."

"Good." She smiled. "I saw you with your mom. I listened to what you said in your speech to your brother and his wife. I think you might be one of the good ones."

I drained the glass, set it on the bar, and she refilled it. "I want what they have," I murmured.

We both turned to look at Abbi and Clay, who were once again on the dance floor, faces shining with love.

"Then, go out and find it," she said. "And remember your promise about getting a ride."

I pulled out my wallet and dropped a fifty in her tip jar. "Well, what-ever-your-name-is, you've given me a lot to think about. So, thanks."

She smiled and then turned to help another customer who'd ambled up to her station.

I looked around the room again.

Abbi, my mom, and my sister were lovely both inside and out. That's what Kara was missing—the internal beauty that went beyond selfishness. The brilliant bartender was right. Kara used her assets to get ahead in the world. But her skin would wrinkle and sag with age, and her body wouldn't be as tight or hot as it was today. Then, she'd have to rely on a personality that left a lot to be desired. When that happened, good luck to her.

I wanted what Clay had with Abbi—what my father was trying to rebuild with my mom.

I wanted *that* kind of love.

So I did the only thing left to me: I walked away. Away from the liquor, away from the easy, meaningless sex, away from the party…from all of it.

I'd take a break and get my head on straight. Then, I could go out and look for a woman, once I knew exactly what I wanted in her.

I headed upstairs to the room my dad insisted I take, glad to crash onto the bed, which I did without bothering to remove my shoes.

I awoke five hours later, thanks to my pounding head. My mouth tasted of cotton dipped in formaldehyde. I made a cup of coffee and showered. As I brushed my teeth, I grimaced at the face that stared back at me in the mirror.

I looked like shit. Part of the reason was because I'd drunk too much but also because I let Kara get to me so deeply. Much as I hated to admit it, I'd planned out my future with her—down to how many kids we'd have—while she planned to drop me for the next best thing.

Making assumptions was frowned upon in my line of work, and clearly should be in my personal life, too.

No one else would be awake this early, so I decided to forgo breakfast with my family and head back to my small, well-appointed apartment near Northwestern's campus.

I bummed around Sunday morning, my head aching too much to do more than flop on the couch and check my social media accounts. I'd defended my dissertation last week. For the first time in what seemed like a decade, I was finished with my responsibilities at Northwestern.

One of my buddies DM'ed me asking if I was okay.

"Why?" I wrote back.

"Just saw Kara's new status. Wanted to make sure you were handling her engagement."

Chapter 3 | Tawny | Sunday

The man who I'd let into my home wanted to kill me.

The moment he pulled the knife from behind his back, I couldn't take my gaze off the glinting sharp edge—not even as I inched along the wall.

I needed to buy some space.

I needed to buy some time.

I needed the possibility of a choice.

Nothing presented itself.

I glanced at the door, and Howie smirked. No way I'd make it, and we both knew it. Not only was he closer, but he also had longer legs, longer arms.

"I could have given you everything, Tawn," he drawled. "I would have given you the world. Hell, if you wanted, I would have married you."

"You came to me with a *job*." I shuddered. "We weren't dating."

Howie shrugged. "I dumped my girlfriend for you. I came here to tell you that." His voice turned wheedling. "I wanted to give us a shot. With your skills and my connections, we could own the world. Literally own it. Kara couldn't give me that." His voice dropped, becoming silkier. "But you could. You *still* can. Just fix that little problem and we'll pretend it never happened."

My mouth dried out, and I shuddered as he stepped closer to

where I was pressed against the wall of my cabin. The man was clearly deranged.

When Howie approached me about a potential job, Agent Russo seemed pleased, telling me I could help lure him in, get more information. He'd told me he'd gotten my name from a colleague, which wasn't unusual. I kept a small stable of clients outside the FBI work to keep up appearances and give me better cover, but I hadn't liked how he seemed to know more about me than I knew about him. That's probably why I'd started looking into his email history as opposed to the firewall.

Well, that and Agent Russo wanted to know everything about Howie. Again, not unusual, but something about this case caused me to feel…cold. I'd been thrilled to send my initial findings to Agent Russo, hoping that would mean my interaction with Howie would be over.

Until he'd shown up a few moments before. And, stupidly, I'd let him into my cabin. I'd been so stupid.

I couldn't take back the messages I'd just attempted to send to Russo even if I wanted to. Hopefully they are already on a secure FBI server, but I didn't get a chance to see if the download was complete. I wanted Howie to pay for his crimes. And for scaring me, and for now wanting me dead.

Like I could ever trust him Not that I ever had, but he'd proven when he'd drawn the blade that there was no way he'd keep his promise to me—the promise that I'd be safe, and we'd be together. No way in hell.

My hand fumbled against the window ledge and my knees weakened. My head swam for a long moment as I nearly sobbed with relief as my finger closed around the latch. It wasn't a door, but if I could give myself a few precious seconds, maybe I could climb out the window. Better make it dive out.

I kept my mouth shut, which was a massive undertaking for me. Not that I was normally talkative—hello, computer geek, here—but I was also curious. Clearly, that saying about curiosity and the cat was true in my current predicament.

I wanted to ask him why he'd cheated the company out of millions of dollars. He'd been cheating for at least six months from what I'd gathered during my weekend of investigating. Probably longer.

Howie was known to be one of Seattle's biggest financial players. No one knew how he'd gotten his money. Except me. I knew how he'd gotten some of it, and now—soon—someone at the FBI did or would…when they read the messages I'd sent to their server.

But that wouldn't help me now. Not with the knife in my face and my cabin located hours from the city and any help that could arrive.

I never should have let Agent Russo talk me into working this case in the first place. Perfectly safe, she'd said.

Well, my ass was about to be sliced up, so I disagreed strongly with Agent Russo's assessment. That damn curiosity again… Agent Russo had raised questions I couldn't ignore that led me to uncover that IP address.

Fine. *Howie* led me to the IP address because, unlike me, Howie wasn't good with technology. I'd used his email account to deposit the door I needed into his company. And all that information was available on the laptop sitting on the end table, mere feet from me. Feet that would put me closer to Howie...and his sharp, scary knife.

Something hit the roof—probably a pinecone—and Howie turned slightly, no doubt to make sure we were still alone—like anyone was coming to save me. Taking advantage of his momentary distraction, I lunged forward and grabbed my laptop. Howie turned back toward me and I swung the computer at his head.

I resisted the urge to check on him and held my computer tightly. It was my evidence—well, my back-up evidence, in case my message didn't go through.

I bolted back to the window, threw it open, and began to wriggle out. The need to turn from my hips to my stomach to fit through the narrow space probably saved my life. I shifted just as a knife blade shredded my jeans and tore across the front of my thigh before clattering to the floor. I screamed in agony.

He'd stabbed me. That cheating, lying asshole stabbed me. Evidently, I hadn't hit him hard enough. I bit my tongue until I tasted blood, unwilling to cry out again or faint from the pain in my thigh.

I pulled my good knee forward and drove my heel back into his chest with as much force as I could manage.

My kick landed on his belly. Howie grunted and stumbled, falling hard against a bookshelf.

I watched as he struck his head against one of the shelves, creating a meaty, head-ache-inducing thunk. Praying this time he wouldn't get back up, I managed to toss out the laptop, then crawl out the window, tumbling to the porch surface in an untidy heap. I gritted my teeth as I staggered to my feet, holding back another sob as pain tore through my leg. The front of my jeans were destroyed, but maybe the wound was superficial?

No such luck.

The slash was a couple of inches above my knee. I couldn't see bone, which was a good sign. The leg could also bear my weight, even though the cut burned and bled with each jostle.

I paused for a moment, allowing some of the dizziness from the shock to pass. My stomach felt like a lead cannonball tied to the world's largest helium balloon. The disconcerting trick to my middle caused more lightheadedness to ensue.

I opened the laptop case, cringing at the creaking noise and unsurprised to find the screen cracked—and blue. Shit. That wasn't good. Not at all. Still, if I were lucky, the hard drive would be intact, and I could remove it from this shell and install it in another.

I closed the case and clutched the machine to me, a talisman of when life was normal and good. I hoped those files went through to the server, but if my hotspot wasn't able to connect and transfer the data before Howie had shown up at my door, then... The answer to that was unclear until I could check.

And here and now wasn't the place or time. Not with Howie planning to cut me to shreds. I shuddered, stomach convulsing at the idea of more of my blood leaving my body.

Think.

I didn't have the keys to my vehicle. And going back in to get them seemed foolhardy. Howie might awaken at any moment. That left walking, either on the path, which I immediately nixed because, again, if Howie woke, he'd easily find me there, or the nearby woods.

Blood saturated my jeans below the cut.

Okay, if my jeans absorbed the blood, then I wouldn't leave an obvious trail. Since I had only my long-sleeved T-shirt on to protect me from the cold December night when it fell in a few hours, I didn't want to tear it up for a bandage unless I had to.

Woods it was, then.

I straightened my spine as I limped into the trees. I'd figure a way out of this conundrum. It was a logic problem, something I excelled at.

At least I used to.

I stumbled through the woods, unwilling to stop, worried I'd fall into shock, even as my legs weighed me to the ground and my shivering increased. My eyes slid closed and I forced them open, just as I forced myself to move forward. I took another step, and another, heedless of the tears streaming down my cheeks.

I needed a drink of water. I needed a blanket. I needed medical attention.

After stumbling my way through the underbrush, for what seemed like forever, I hit the narrow strip of Highway 101 that would eventually lead out to Lake Quinault. Unfortunately, that just led me deeper into the Olympic Peninsula, and more exposed to Howie's violence when he found me. *If* he found me. I shuddered and gagged as my mind replayed the crack of his head against the bookshelf.

Safety. I needed to be safe. I stood for a moment before turning south. Seattle. The FBI. That was my best chance. I began to walk close to the road, but not too close. I needed to be able to dart back into the woods at the first sound of a vehicle.

I stumbled again. So tired. My limbs and lids must weigh thousands of pounds.

I'd never been hurt before—violence was new to me, and I really, really didn't like participating in it.

"I'm a statistic," I muttered. "A domestic violence number."

My toes caught under a root and I tripped, sprawling. I cried out as my wounded leg jarred against the ground. I managed to turn so I landed on my shoulder, protecting my laptop from the brunt of the fall. I couldn't lose the work there. It was my ticket out of this mess—my best chance to finally leave this work and head out to Wyoming.

I'd made promises to my mom, and I really wanted to keep them. But I had to complete this project to be in a position to follow through.

My mother lived in Laramie now and needed help, sandwiched as she was between her ill parents and the kids she'd started fostering a few years ago.

We hadn't spoken in years, but she had reached out to me a while back and now she wanted my help. And I wanted to give it, to prove to her I was more than the mistakes of my past. But that meant getting up and walking.

Except I couldn't manage to rise again. I was tired and cold and scared.

This wasn't what I'd signed up for.

I snorted. I didn't get to decide what I'd do for the Bureau. That was what I'd signed up for: to do whatever they needed.

I had less than three months left on my contract. If I could survive this case.

But Howie wasn't going to let me go—not without trying to silence me again. Fear and shock overwhelmed me, and my eyes slid closed.

Chapter 4 | Colt | Sunday

"Kara's engaged? That can't be right," I said. "She told me last night that her live-in boyfriend dumped her."

"That's what her social media says—engaged. Wait. Wow, that was quick. Married."

"What the actual… You know what? I don't care."

Except her words, the desperate look in her eye, rankled. Why would she come to me last night?

To make her boyfriend, Hugh or Harry or whatever it is, jealous. Dammit. She'd used me again. Apparently, to get engaged.

That hurt. Again. Even more evidence I needed to get off this Kara-train and focus my life.

Instead of waiting for opportunities to come to me, I needed to search them out. I'd considered heading out to my family's cabin last night. There wouldn't be a better time than now.

I pulled out a suitcase and slammed it on the bed. Some of the residual anger and shame from my encounter with Kara seeped into my motions as I threw clothes in willy-nilly, much against my normal fastidious manner. Underwear, socks, sweatpants, jeans, T-shirts, and a couple of sweatshirts. Oh, and a coat. The water by the cabin always made the temperature feel cooler. I grabbed my favorite down jacket, a beanie, and some gloves and shoved them in the top of the bag along with a pair of sneakers and my hiking boots.

There. I could spend a week or more out at the cabin and think through my goals and where I wanted my life to go.

First order of business: time to start living my life. I'd chill for a few days while I came up with my perfect-woman list.

I hauled the bag down to my car.

———

I glared at the setting sun about an hour later, which had the audacity to settle right into my still-hungover-as-hell eyeballs.

"Fuck," I moaned. "Stupid bright star. My head is never going to be the same."

It had been hours since I heard the news. I should be feeling better by now. But I wasn't, and I refused to consider my physical lamentations had anything to do with Kara's engagement.

So what if she'd tried to wheedle back into my good graces? So what if she'd lied—tried to manipulate me to her will *again*?

We'd broken up ages ago. She'd moved on. I had, too, and I'd proven that last night.

Now, I needed to consider this job in Laramie. Cassidy was in remission. My parents...well, I wasn't sure what they were, but it wasn't as if I'd be able to fix their relationship, no matter how much I wanted to.

And Clay was married to his soul mate. He was settled, happy.

He had everything I'd ever wanted, and he'd thumbed his nose at...at least until he met Abbi.

Not his fault that he found love first. Maybe it wasn't in the cards for me. Much as I hated to consider that option, I feared I'd end up as that weird, forgetful professor that students whispered about. I pondered this possibility, not liking that future.

Maybe what I really needed was to shake up my situation.

That's when I saw the body on the edge of the highway.

Chapter 5 | Colt | Sunday

"Be a deer, be a deer," I whispered, even as my palms began to sweat, and my heart slammed against my ribs. "Or a mountain lion. Or…"

I trailed off because the long, tangled honey-colored hair was clearly attached to a human head, and, as I inched closer, I ascertained that the body attached to that head and hair was in the shape of a woman.

A small one, maybe even tinier than my little sister. She wasn't dressed for the winter chill.

I pulled over, trying to swallow past the dryness in my mouth as I pocketed the car keys. Not what I had in mind when I thought about shaking up my situation. I'd been considering online dating.

Whatever this was, it was way outside my area of expertise. I exited the vehicle, taking slow, measured steps toward her. I gulped down the fear that sizzled in my guts.

"Um… Miss?"

No response.

My stomach iced over. What if she were dead? Had she been hit by a car? I leaned down and noted the bloodstain around her thigh.

Shit. That couldn't be good. I tugged at the edge of her pants and grimaced at the sight of her ragged flesh.

All right. An injury of this magnitude I could deal with. It was above her knee and long—but it wasn't too deep, through the outer layer of flesh, and the edges of the wound had already begun to scab over. I headed back to my car and pulled out a T-shirt. I ripped it into long strips and then made a pad out of the remainder. I placed the pad against her leg and then wrapped the strips around her thigh, securing the knots.

"No. Don't touch me," she said. The words were a moaning whisper, a bit too thready. "You hurt me, Howie."

Howie? The only Howie I knew was engaged…no…married to Kara.

A chill licked its way down my spine. I rejected the connection because I'd seen Kara less than twenty-four hours before in Seattle, and she'd managed to ensnare *her* Howie in wedlock during that time. Sure, I'd driven a couple of hours to the peninsula, but it was unlikely either Kara or her Howie were here.

That was the logical answer. But…something low in my belly continued to fire off a sizzle of warning.

Based on what little I could infer from her situation, whoever stabbed her must have then left her on the side of the road. Or she'd escaped him and ended up here.

Either option caused rage to boil up hard and fast in my chest. I glanced around, hoping to find this Howie schmuck so I could shove my fist in his face.

Nothing—not a person or creature that I could see. Just trees and the road, and now my headlights illuminating the woman as twilight had fallen during my drive. The beams created deep shadows in the surrounding low-lying area near the trees.

She clutched something to her chest—a laptop. I grasped it, ready to pull it from her hands.

She opened her eyes and shrieked.

I fell back on my butt, her ear-piercing scream still ringing in my head.

"Don't touch me. Don't touch my computer." Her voice remained wispy. She needed fluids, and a few stitches wouldn't hurt, but I didn't think the injury was life-threatening.

"Hey, I'm just trying to help you," I said. "You're bleeding."

Her teeth chattered, clicking so hard they had to hurt. How long had she been out there?

"He...he s-s-stabbed me," she said. Her eyes were wide—an unusual, warm gold. Like the amber pendant that housed a perfectly preserved dragonfly that I'd given my mother one year.

I'd been a total science geek pretty much from the crib. My parents, being awesome, supported my passions instead of trying to push me into music or some other art.

None of the interests that came so easily to Clay or my teen-aged sister, Cassidy, had sat well on my shoulders. Music and creativity left me itchy and uncomfortable like a horsehair blanket.

"Where is this guy—Howie?" I asked, glancing around again so I didn't fall back into her eyes. "Is he after you?"

"M-maybe." Her jaw shivered and her teeth clacked.

I winced.

"How'd you end up here?" I shook my head. "Never mind. Let's get you in my car. It's warm, and we can call the police."

"No," she said. She lunged forward and grabbed my wrist, her face a grimace of pain, but her eyes pleading. She glanced around.

"What time is it?"

"About five-thirty."

She blew out a breath. "What day?"

"Sunday," I said. That bad feeling congealed in my belly.

"Okay. Good."

"Why?"

"Because Howie showed up about two this afternoon, so that means I left my place a couple of hours ago, maybe. I was worried because it's dark now, and I wasn't sure how long I'd been unconscious."

"Let's get you up. In my car. Then, we can call—"

"Not the police."

My hand was halfway toward her, but I stopped extending it and blinked at the finality of her tone. "Yes, the police."

She shook her head, adamant. "Not happening."

"That's who you call when you find stabbed women on the side of the road."

I was impatient. What was wrong with this woman? Had she hit her head? Or maybe she just wasn't very bright.

No matter what the reason, I couldn't leave her. I'd just have to figure out a way to contact the proper authorities. And soon. Because I did not want to deal with her any longer than necessary.

"We'll talk to law enforcement personnel after I see what transmitted," she said. She tried to pull herself upright and failed, her mouth pressed in a tight line.

I caught her wrist and used my other hand under her elbow. I helped her upright and she stumbled, falling against my chest.

I'd been right—she was tiny. Smaller than Cassidy, who barely topped five-three.

"Promise me," she said as she held onto my shirt. I wrapped my arm around her waist and started walking toward my car.

"Promise you what?"

"That you'll wait for me to tell you when it's safe to call."

Safe? The hair at my nape rose and that inky blackness refilled my low belly. Why was she talking like she was in a spy novel?

"Erm, we need to get you some medical attention," I said.

Each step clearly caused her agony. Sweat broke out along her upper lip, and her face paled. "After I get an internet connection. That's first. In fact, it's paramount."

She didn't talk like an imbecile. So…why didn't she want me calling the police?

"Are you involved in something nefarious?" I asked.

"Define nefarious," she hedged.

Well, shit.

"Are you in trouble with the law?" I asked.

Her grip loosened and her gaze darted away. Should I let her run back into the woods? No, I'd worry about her. She was injured. And she was small. Darkness had fallen fast and silent between one blink and another, leaving her more at risk.

I didn't want her attacked by a bear. Or Howie.

She took another step and her foot caught on a rock, causing her leg to buckle. With a soft gasp, her eyes rolled back, and she collapsed against me, totally out, but still gripping the damn computer. Clearly, whatever was on it mattered to her.

A lot.

The underbrush rustled nearby, and I turned, all the hair on my body standing on end. I studied the spot, half expecting a psycho named Howie to dart out of the trees, brandishing a knife.

Nothing happened.

My head pounded. *How the hell did I end up in this crazy-ass situation?*

I blew out a breath and turned my gaze back to the fine-boned woman lying in the light of my high beams.

No way I could leave her.

So, that left me with a couple of shitty choices: call 9-1-1 against her wishes and let them deal with her, or somehow get her into my car and take her to the cabin with me.

Dammit. I wanted to believe her. I berated myself, trying to point out I'd just realized I needed to steer clear of women...or at least have a much better sense of what would make a good life partner. That's part of what I was supposed to be doing out here, at the cabin. Figuring out my future—trying to go after what I wanted.

Against my better judgment, I scooped her into my arms. She was light, maybe too light. As I stood, the laptop began to tumble from her grasp, but I managed to catch it. Barely. I settled it in her lap, once again surprised by how small she was.

I'd always gone for statuesque women with plump curves. But this woman was the opposite. She reminded me of the fairies Cassidy obsessed over during her treatments. I'd read to her about the pixie people as she struggled to keep the chemotherapy drugs in her system.

I never thought I'd be nostalgic for those moments we'd shared, but something about this woman in my arms reminded me of those memories—in the best possible way.

After some finagling, that had me opening the hatchback and setting her just inside the SUV, I grabbed one of my sweatshirts from the bag in the back and spread it out on the passenger seat. Then, I walked back to the cargo area and picked her up. With a sigh, I lowered the woman onto the seat, making sure the sweatshirt was under her thigh.

I really hoped I hadn't just managed to aid and abet a criminal. With my shitty luck, especially with women, who knew.

Chapter 6 | Tawny | Sunday

My memories perforated after I left the cabin. I'd walked, clasping my laptop, praying the information made it through, worrying it hadn't. Mostly, though, I felt terror that Howie was just behind me, about to thrust his blade through my back.

Or...maybe worse, that he was dead. Because of me. That thought rolled through my head over and over as I'd limped and dragged myself out of the woods and toward the highway. I needed a phone—mine was still in the cabin, thanks to my speedy departure—and I needed a safe place to lay low until I could talk to the FBI agent I'd been working with on this case.

Neither appeared achievable and both were made more difficult thanks to my aching leg.

When I'd fallen over—more like passed out, and it wasn't the easy, graceful descent that I'd seen on TV—I'd managed to stumble closer to the road. I'd awoken practically on the asphalt. I shuddered, and not just because of my aches from my tumble into unconsciousness. If a driver had come around the curve just right, or hadn't been paying attention, I'd be dead.

Instead, I came to with a gorgeous man in jeans and a hoodie crouched over me. His presence made me feel safe. He was big and warm and real and his hands gentle. Tears came to my eyes at his kindness. This proved a night of firsts: Howie abused me and now, mere hours later, a sexy stranger played my white knight. The change in the men around me caused my head to spin.

My cheeks burned as I realized I'd passed out for a second time. He must have carried me to his car since I woke up in a seat.

That was kind. And he had the best eyes. They'd been concerned as he met my gaze. Concerned and, and…nice. A pretty hazel color, offset by the tumble of his dark, unruly hair.

None of the cold calculation my colleagues and targets all shared.

So what? He was nice. And pretty. Very…pretty wasn't the right word for him. If I'd had time to write an algorithm of my perfect man, it would have given me this one. Not that I wrote those kinds of programs, or that I'd even really talked to any man, who wasn't connected to this investigation, in months. I frowned as I considered everything I'd postponed for the past few years, all for the Federal Bureau of Investigation.

And what had the agents done for me?

So far, they'd asked me to work in a drab cubicle some of the time, but once Howie contacted me, Russo suggested I stay home. She had one of her minions check in three times a week to make sure I was still working. Again, that niggle of something odd occurring. Something I didn't have all the data to understand.

Because Agent Russo didn't appear concerned about my safety, I hadn't understood how dangerous Howie was.

Apparently, some people would do literally anything for money. I had no doubt Howie would have followed through on his threat to kill me if I hadn't gotten in a well-placed kick.

I shuddered. I didn't want my life to be based on luck and

odds. That seemed...well, playing with my life like that was sheer stupidity. Because, probably soon, I wouldn't be fast enough or smart enough or *whatever* enough to escape.

And then I'd be dead.

This stranger smelled good. *Really* good. And he made me feel safe, which was strange. Mainly because I hadn't even felt physically unsafe until today. Maybe that was why I made the connection to this guy. He'd bound my wound. He'd been kind enough to bring me into the safety of his vehicle.

But I didn't know him, and he could be working for Howie.

Shit.

I'd mentioned Howie by name. Could I be any stupider? For all I knew, he was taking me back to Howie so he could actually kill me.

But I didn't get a killer vibe. In fact, the hot guy in the hoodie, my rescuer, made me think of home.

Which made me even more confused.

Because I hadn't had a home in years. Sure, I had a place to live, but it wasn't home. That had disappeared after my dad died.

I passed out again before I could say anything stupid.

Chapter 7 | Tawny | Sunday

I woke to the man popping the button open on my jeans. My hand came up to cover his, but I missed, my arm leaden and fingers numb. I stared up at the roof of a vehicle.

"Whoa, there, tiger. We don't know each other's names yet," I slurred.

What was wrong with me?

Right. Blood loss. Cold temperatures. I must be in shock.

Shivers racked my body, causing me to grit my teeth against the pain in my fingers and the worse pain in my thigh.

His lips tipped up before he went back to pulling at my pants. "I promise, I'm not going to molest you."

"Good to know you'd ask first," I said. I blinked at him, frowning at my words. I wasn't usually this forward with men. I preferred to watch, to analyze, to ensure I understood the situation before I inserted myself into it.

Look where that got me with Howie. A painful slash on the thigh and near-death by exposure. I was pretty sure my time unconscious outside had been worse for my health than the stabbing, but I really wished I hadn't experienced either.

He met my gaze briefly, his serious. "Always. I need to look at the wound more closely. See if you need stitches. I won't try anything further that'll make you uncomfortable."

"The idea of you seeing me pant-less makes me uncomfortable," I muttered.

And it did, but not exactly for the reasons I implied. Besides my obvious and already categorized problems, I probably smelled of fear and exertion. Nothing about me was attractive or sexy. And the guy kneeling in front of me was both those things—and then some.

Figured that I'd meet an attractive man during my lowest point. Unfair? Absolutely, So, that was why I should have expected it.

"Cuz I'm in no position to fight back."

He raised his gaze to mine, holding it, letting me see how serious he was before he spoke. And when he did, those words washed over me in a powerful rush.

"I promise on my sister's continued good health that I won't ever take advantage of you or hurt you. I need to check out your wound because you've bled through the bandage I made for you."

I held onto his hand a little tighter.

"What's your name? I think I should know it before you see me in my panties."

He smiled. "I'm Colt."

"Locked and loaded. Like the revolver," I said.

"That's really disconcerting, hearing you talk like that. You look like you're the same age as my baby sister."

His voice was a rumbling bass. That song "I'm Too Sexy" started playing in my head, and I struggled to keep from humming along. Again, I blamed my weird reaction to shock. Because it surely wasn't logical.

"I'm in shock so you can't hold me accountable for anything I say right now. And I'm twenty-nine," I said.

"My sister is sixteen."

"Yeah, well, I guess looks are deceiving," I said. "My name is Tawny Reed."

"Nice to meet you, Tawny. Now, will you please let me look at your thigh?"

I removed my hand from where it covered his. I groaned when he pulled the cloth away from my leg. Glancing down at the angry, ugly gash, I hissed as blood trickled from the wound.

"Damn him for his greed."

"Him being the ass who stabbed you? Howie, you said?"

"None other," I said.

My pants pooled around my ankles while blood seeped into a sweatshirt he must have placed under my legs. I closed my eyes and tilted my head up to stare at the SUV's ceiling. There was a sunroof, currently closed. I was glad because my teeth started to chatter again.

"Are you a doctor?" I asked. That would make sense. A hot doc looking to relax for a weekend away. He saves a damsel in distress. They live happily ever after.

I frowned. That sounded like a terrible storyline—one I wanted no part of because I was *not* going to be a distressed damsel. I could take care of myself. I pointed out that I was alive and getting help, so clearly I was capable of maintaining my own life.

"I'm a doctor, yes."

"What's your specialty?"

"Microbiology."

I jerked. "Not medicine?" I asked, peering at him from the

corner of my eye.

A faint flush heated his cheeks. "Sorry to disappoint you, but no. I have a Ph.D., not an MD."

"Not well-versed in trauma, huh?" I asked. "Like, in the ER?"

"I've never seen a stabbing, no, but I have spent years of my life cutting into animals."

He met my gaze briefly, and maybe he saw the flicker of alarm that sped through me. Of course this dude was too good to be true. Of course he hurt animals.

"Dissections, Tawny."

"I said that out loud."

"You did. And now I've learned you jump to conclusions," he said. "I'm a biology and chemistry doctor."

"Both, huh? A minute ago it was just microbiology. I feel like maybe you're not being totally honest with me."

He raised his hands enough for me to see them shaking. "Well, I just defended my doctoral dissertation so it's a brand new occurrence. And this past hour has been surreal. I'm doing my best with absolutely no support, background, or help from said person-in-need." The last was delivered with a severe scowl.

"Sorry. I'm sorry. I've had a really bad day. What with getting stabbed. And then having to walk through the woods. I thought animals were attracted to the smell of blood, and the idea of coming up on a bear freaked me out."

"Bears are day predators," Colt murmured. He poked at the edges of my wound. "They would have been out earlier, when you started walking, but, by now, most are in their dens. And this isn't too deep, so while I know it has to hurt, it's not trauma—as in, you won't die at any second."

I yelped and shifted, trying to get away from the ripples of discomfort in my thigh.

"Stay still."

"That hurt," I said.

"I'm not surprised. But I can't help you if you're jumping around so much that I can't get this antibiotic cream on the cut. I don't think you have to have stitches, but they'd probably ensure less of a scar and help it heal faster."

He glanced up at me, waiting.

"I can't go to the hospital," I said softly. "Not until I..." I trailed off. I shouldn't share more with Colt.

He shook his head. "Why am I not surprised you're being difficult? Fine. But don't say I didn't warn you."

"Got it." I floundered for a moment, trying to find a different track for our conversation. "A doctor of both microbiology and chemistry, huh? That's impressive. And better than being a weirdo who cuts into animals for kicks."

"You say strange things," he said as he sat back, pulling something out of his bundle. He began to rip the cotton into strips. Ah, a T-shirt. He folded the leftover third into a pad and placed it against my wound.

"I'm not going to have any shirts left by the time I get you where you need to go," he muttered.

"Why's that?"

"This is the second shirt I've ripped up and your sitting on another."

"Right. I bled through the first."

He wound the longer strips around my leg, securing the pieces. "Which had me worried, especially since you were unconscious, but it also probably cleaned out any dirt and bad bacteria from the wound. A tetanus shot wouldn't hurt either."

"Tetanus? I don't want that?"

"When did you get your last shot?"

"Um…a couple of years ago. Yeah. Three. I stepped on a staple." At his look, I waved my hand. "I like to be barefoot. Well, I used to before I got a thick wad of staples to my heel."

He winced.

My mind grew a bit fuzzier. "I'm not normally this weird. I mean, I'm shy, and I prefer code to people, so I'm weird. Anti-social, even, and clearly awkward around hot guys."

I bit my lips, sucking them into my mouth.

He smirked, his amused gaze darting up to mine, but thankfully didn't comment.

"Well, you're not the only one feeling weird. I've been sitting here, trying to decide if I was aiding and abetting a criminal. I'm in a bit of a conundrum."

"I'm not a criminal," I said, my back stiffening. "My father was a decorated officer of the law."

He had been, until that last mission, anyway. No way I was going to bring *that* up, though.

"Not sure what, exactly, that has to do with *your* willingness to follow the rules, but that's cool." He hesitated. "My dad's a musician."

"That's nice," I said. "Are you finished? I'll get out of your vehicle and head back toward the town."

He kept his eyes on the makeshift bandage on my leg. Finally, he stopped tinkering and placed his hand on my knee. I jerked, shocked by the sudden warmth of his palm on my skin.

"I'm assuming I can trust you, Tawny."

I nibbled at my lower lip. "Well, I could say the same about you. I mean, since you took the time to bandage me."

He shook his head. "I'm not letting you walk like this. Where to?"

"What?"

"Where do you want to go?" he asked, looking at me like I was a simpleton.

He rose from the ground, shut my door, and headed around the front to the driver's side. He settled his long body in the seat and clicked his seatbelt into place. I continued to watch as he pressed the ignition button next to the steering wheel.

"Where's my computer?" I asked, suddenly panicked. No way I was leaving without it.

He pointed to the space at my feet. I bent down, trying to ignore the pull of my cut, and placed it in my lap. I sighed with relief, thankful to have it in my hands once more.

"Where do you need me to drive you?" he asked again.

I clutched the edges of the laptop so hard that I could feel indentations digging deeply into my palms. "I need to get away from the highway. If…" I shuddered. "If Howie can get to his car, he'll come looking for me."

"If?" Colt asked.

I sucked in a deep, ragged breath.

"I kicked him after he stabbed me. He fell back into my

bookcase."

I glanced down at my lap, at the machine that had become so important. Colt's deep sigh pretty much summed up the entirety of the situation.

"So *he* may need medical attention?"

I shrugged. Howie definitely needed attention—legal for sure, maybe medical. Fine, probably medical.

He grunted. "We'll head toward my cabin. That's where I was going when I saw you. There's a town between here and there. Once we get to the town, you can do your shit, and I can get some answers." He scrubbed his palms over his face, and I heard the faint rasp of whiskers. That delectable five-o-clock shadow made me shiver.

"What do you do, Tawny?" he asked.

I managed to pull my scattered thoughts together. "Do? You mean for work?"

"Yes, that's exactly what I mean."

He shot me a look with eyebrows lowered, like I was the weird one. Okay, maybe I was. But... I was having a really bad day.

"I'm an ethical hacker," I said.

"Really?" he asked, his tone making it clear he didn't believe me.

I straightened my spine and glared at him.

"Yes, *really*. Why would I lie about my job?"

"Maybe because I've yet to get a straight or full answer out of you about...anything."

"I told you about my dad," I said, huffing as I flopped back against the seat. "And I don't like to talk about him."

"And you expect me to believe that?"

"Yes," I said. "Because it's the truth."

"So, you want me to believe that an ethical hacker just happened to be deep in the woods on the Olympic Peninsula—where Wi-Fi is nearly impossible to get—and you just happened to get stabbed and you just happened to have collapsed on the side of the road and you just happened to…what are you going to tell me next? You work for the CIA? FBI? NSA?" He raised an eyebrow.

Great. He didn't trust me. No doubt he thought I was feeding him lines of BS and planned to dump me at the nearest police station.

I straightened my spine. Fine. That would get me out of his care and closer to the authorities who could help me.

"I appreciate the ride to town," I said, my tone stilted. "I'll get out of your way as soon as we're there, and I can talk to the county sheriff, do a little war-driving if I need to."

Colt had pulled the car onto the road and now he turned to glare at me. "War-driving?"

"Driving around until I can find a decent Wi-Fi signal I can hack into."

"You don't have a car," he pointed out.

"You do."

"Do you make a habit of doing that?" he asked.

"Not a habit, no." Though I had managed to use my cell phone data to create a hotspot, which should have forwarded the information, including my suggestion for a time bomb into the backdoor I'd found in Shasta Aeronautics' network. I'd made that suggestion based on my initial meeting with Howie last week, and the feeling about him intensified when he followed me to my cabin. Howie wouldn't have done that if he wasn't desperate. But desperate from what? He said he wanted to keep potential enemies out of his private equity's investment, but I hadn't seen external breaches, which led me to believe the problems were coming from within his firm or Shasta itself. The time bomb would detonate and give us an opportunity to track all further correspondences. At least, that was my hope.

I tapped my fingers on the laptop case, hoping the message had cleared my hot spot before I closed my machine when Howie had arrived.

"Did you say you know the sheriff?" Colt asked. He probably didn't want to ask more questions about my current job—no doubt he thought I was really a cracker.

I might have been at one time, but no one could accuse me of that now. Though, I felt, at times, I was more of a gray-hat for the FBI. There were times I questioned if the information I managed to compile would be permissible in the courtroom.

Russo never told me, and I'd learned not to ask questions. Mainly because I didn't like the answers Russo gave me.

My smile was tight and tiny. "He was my dad's partner."

"Was?"

"My father's dead."

Chapter 8 | Colt | Sunday

This chick was feeding me lies on top of whoppers. How stupid did she think I was? She studied me from the corner of her eye, no doubt realizing I planned to make a call—and get her out of my vehicle as soon as possible. Had I told her too much about myself?

I was worried she'd focus on me, maybe stab me. She could have hurt herself. I had no clue why my mind went there, just that I wasn't comfortable about her explanation, and much worse, I was attracted to her. Dirty and injured, she still managed to turn me on, which caused deep disappointment in myself.

"Do you have a signal?" she asked, wrenching me out of my self-castigation.

"I don't know. Why?"

"I'll make a call, right now."

"To?" I asked.

"The sheriff you don't think I know."

"How do I know that's who you call?"

She threw her arms up in the air. "Are you always this skeptical?" she groused.

"No." My lips twitched because her frustration was cute. "You bring it out of me."

"How about logic? Aren't science-y people supposed to be logical?"

"That's part of why I don't want to give you my phone. Logic tells me you could call someone who's going to hurt me. Or put a virus on it."

"Then you look up the sheriff's number and dial it. Ask for Hemp."

I frowned at her, trying to figure out her angle, but I pulled to the side of the empty road and did as she asked. I connected the call via my Bluetooth system in case I needed my hands.

"Grays Harbor sheriff's office. This is Hemp," said a deep voice a moment later.

"My name is Colten Rippey, and I have a woman named Tawny Reed with me. Do you know her?"

"Yeah, of course. Is she okay?"

"Mostly—"

"Hemp, I'm fine. Please don't yell at him," Tawny said, speaking loudly over the sheriff's angry voice.

"You in a scrape, Tawn? How'd you manage that? Weren't you supposed to be working that aviation case for Agent Russo?"

"I am. But I ran into some trouble," she said. "Howie Novak showed up at my cabin a few hours ago."

I startled at the name. That *was* the same man Kara dumped me for—her brand-new husband, if what my friend said was true. The same man Tawny said attacked her.

Should I mention that to the sheriff? Not yet. I wasn't completely sure who Tawny was. Or what she was to the man on the other end of the phone. Ensuring my own survival leaped to the front of my current list of to-dos.

Sharing possible speculative information? Not so much.

My grip on the steering wheel slipped, thanks to my sweaty palms. I corrected our course, getting us back on the road, and Tawny hissed out a breath when her thigh bounced.

"Your place?"

"Yeah. I never told him about it, so I'm kinda freaked out he drove out here to find me."

"You need to tell him where and how I found you," I said.

"There's more?" Hemp asked.

"Yeah. Um. He stabbed me."

The line went quiet. Too quiet. "This Colten Rippey man stabbed you?"

The voice drifting through the airwaves was sinister. I shuddered. Staying on this guy's good side just jumped close to the top of my to-do list.

"No, no," she said in a placating voice. "He rescued me. Howie stabbed me. And, well, I fought him off. He hit my bookshelf—you know the one that separates the living room from the kitchen area? I think it fell on him, but I didn't stick around to find out because…well, he'd just stabbed me."

"How bad is it? Where are you? I'll send an ambulance."

"I'm okay. We're about…"

She looked at me. "Where are we?" she asked.

"We're about fifteen miles from Montesano."

"You get that, Hemp?" At his affirmative, Tawny said, "Maybe you could have someone check out my place, see if Howie's still there. And I'll need to make a call to Agent Russo. I don't think she'd appreciate me giving Colt that number."

"Will do, Tawn. I'll get a guy out there stat and meet you in the Beehive diner lot. You know that place? It's hard to miss. I'll get you back to Seattle."

"Thanks, Hemp. I'm sure Colt's happy to hear he can get rid of me soon."

The connection broke as Hemp hung up.

No, I wasn't actually eager to see her go. Now that I had confirmation she'd been telling the truth, her story fascinated me. Who was this Agent Russo? What group did she work for? I'd mentioned a few of the big agencies. And the aviation deal—what was that?

"You mentioned aviation."

She frowned. "*I* didn't. Hemp did."

"Is that what Howie's involved in? Listen, my brother and his new wife were supposed to board a flight soon. If there's some way they're in danger, I have to warn them." Panic gnawed at my guts. "This is my family. *Please.*"

She worried her lip so hard, I worried she'd draw blood. "I'm not supposed to talk about it. I signed an NDA. If Agent Russo finds out—"

I turned to look at her, slowing the car and coming to a stop in the middle of the road. "I can't let something happen to Clay."

"I don't know," she said. "That's what I've been trying to figure out. I'm pretty sure Howie and his associates are selling subpar replacement parts to smaller airliners and pocketing the difference. But I haven't proved that yet, just skirted some emails—"

"What kind of small airliners?" I asked.

Her brows tightened over her nose and she gave me a quizzical look. "Like private jets. So, as long as your brother is on a commercial flight, he'll be fine."

All the blood drained from my face. "He's not flying commercial. God, Tawny, what if his plane goes down?"

Her face drained of color. "What type is he flying?"

"Why can't you just tell me?" I demanded.

"Zephyr," she whispered, pressing back against the door. "And possibly a few others—all American-made. But I've been able to find a trail between Shasta Aeronautics and Zephyr Corporate Jets that suggests…"

She abruptly stopped, probably because she realized she was about to say too much. I pulled over and stopped, so we weren't in the middle of the road, already working through my contact list. Tawny grabbed my wrist and I raised my gaze, glaring.

"This situation has to be handled delicately," she said, enunciating each word.

"Have you thought for a moment that people could *die*? Like, blow up in the sky, and you had the information to prevent it? This isn't The Trolley Question from a philosophy textbook. These are people with lives and families, many of whom are counting on them not just to earn a living but to, you know, be in their lives."

"Look, I have a job to do," she said. She winced as if—even to her—that sounded pathetic. "One that requires me to remain within a strict code of ethics and guidelines…"

I snorted, the derision suffocating.

"So do I. To protect *my family*. If you aren't on board with that, I can let you out here."

She squinted. "You'd leave an injured woman on the side of

the road?"

"You'd let my brother die because some ongoing investigation matters more to you?"

She shrank into the seat, gaze turning out the window. "I can see your logic."

She looked out the window and stifled a gasp.

"What?" I asked.

She pointed into the distance. "Do you see that? Are those... are those *flames*?"

I glanced up, unconcerned by the growing plume of gray-black smoke boiling up into the sky. The conflagration was visible against the inky blackness, and it was in a section of woods nearby.

"So? This is Washington. A wildfire isn't exactly uncommon."

"In December?" she asked, matching my sarcasm. "And pretty much in the *exact* location of where my cabin is located?"

Chapter 9 | Colt | Sunday

"Are you sure?" I asked as my body wound tighter than a coiled spring.

"Positive."

"You think someone tried to burn down the cabin?" I asked.

"Sure looks that way."

"The guy Hemp was sending? Do you think—"

"No, couldn't have gotten there fast enough."

Tawny looked paler than she had before, and her delicate throat bobbed. "This scheme Howie's involved in…there are hundreds of millions of dollars at stake and people's continued freedom, including his. So, would he burn down my place to try and protect those details? Yes."

Christ. I'd tried to do a good deed—pick up a woman from the side of the road. Stop her bleeding. Now, I was smack in the middle of some kind of terrible conspiracy. My head pounded from the strain of the past hour.

"Freedom?" I asked.

Her face seemed to sag a little, as if the weight of the situation wanted to drag her under.

"These crimes I've started to uncover are serious felonies. If the FBI can help prove people have intentionally risked others' lives to enrich themselves, then they won't see the outside of a prison again, no matter how good or expensive their lawyer is."

"And how did you get involved in this, Tawny?"

Her lashes fluttered as her gaze fell back to her lap. "That's a long story. Bottom line: I'm working with the FBI. And I'm going to be in a lot of trouble for sharing any information with you."

"Agent Russo is your contact?"

"I report to her. I sent her my findings earlier—"

"As in, before you got the knife wound and before…" I scrubbed my hands down my face.

I studied the young woman holding the laptop. She did seem to have an unnatural devotion to the machine.

"I didn't expect the simple hack-job to turn into something so big and potentially dangerous. I had no idea how it would expand. I didn't understand…"

"How'd you get involved?"

She hesitated. "He approached me."

"Approached you?"

"He wanted me to look into his security, but then the deal seemed to change. I don't know if he realized I was delving into their past communications, but when he came out here to my cabin, he made it sound like he'd throw in a romantic arrangement if I was willing to do what he wanted."

No wonder Kara came back to me. She must be aware of Howie's wandering eye. And Kara wasn't one to share. Ironic that she'd cheated on me with Howie only to have him at least attempt to do the same to her—for similar reasons. Greed wasn't something I understood. But then, I'd never had to worry about money.

And I preferred my lab to people.

"He wanted to sleep with you and get you to…what? Work for him?" I asked.

"Yes. Well, maybe. He'd asked me to close any possible loopholes in their servers—to tighten up their cyber security. I agreed because Agent Russo asked me to, but she asked me to push deeper since I had access to their servers."

"Ergo, the FBI suspected him of something."

It sounded like no one had explained the risks of the assignment she'd been given, and Tawny, who seemed a bit shy and naive, hadn't realized the danger, so she hadn't been able to calculate the risks to her safety. Either that, or she was playing me better than a guitar solo at the Grammys.

Or Kara had screwed me up when she screwed me over last year, and I now had trust issues.

Scratch that. I definitely had trust issues. Did that mean I could trust Tawny? Should I?

And could I live with myself if I didn't and something bad happened to her?

Rock meet hard place.

I stared at her bandaged thigh, pleased to see no new blood had leaked through the cotton. I caught her watching me. Her cheeks bloomed with color, and I exhaled the entirety of the breath I'd been holding. If she could blush, she must not be in imminent danger.

Christ. That was a stupid thought. I was the proud recipient of a Ph.D. in biology. I, more than anyone, understood the circulatory system.

"It's too late for me to back out of this," she said. "I... I'm scared."

"Can't you hand over the laptop?"

She hesitated. "Well, yes, but it was supposed to upload to an encrypted server. That's why I need to call. To make sure."

"And if it didn't?" I asked.

Again, she hesitated. "Once I get to a place with Wi-Fi and can check—as long as the hard drive wasn't destroyed when I hit Howie in the face with it."

The realization slammed into my face, right between the eyes. Tawny might well have the only copy of the incriminating information. Which made that laptop extremely valuable.

She mumbled something about removing the hard drive and the need for proper equipment to do so. She stared down at the machine. She seemed to reach a decision with a slight nod.

Until that information was transferred and reviewed, and until arrests were made, Tawny's life was in danger.

Chapter 10 | Colt | Sunday

"I need to call Clay."

She nodded but I'd already called up his number and pressed the talk button. As the call connected, I ensured my phone didn't connect to my car's Bluetooth speakers.

"H'lo?" he said, clearly more asleep than awake.

"Clay, don't get on that plane," I said.

"What? Colt? Are you okay? You disappeared last night. We were all worried about you."

"I'm fine. Kind of in the middle of something—"

"Please tell me it isn't Kara," Clay said.

"What? No. That's never going to happen. Look, I'm calling because I found out...something..." I glanced over at Tawny, who gazed at me with pleading eyes. "Don't get on the plane today. It's...there could be problems."

"Bit late, bro. We took a private jet to Fiji last night, courtesy of Hayden and Abbi's Aunt Briar."

"And you made it? You're okay?" I asked, the worry deflating and allowing me to breathe fully. Weird sensation.

"Yeah, we arrived...shit, like thirty minutes ago. At our hut or whatever. This place is slick. We're actually on the water. Not next to it. I can see the ocean through the floor."

"And you're there for ten days?"

"Yeah. I told you that weeks ago and again last night. Colt, you said you're in the middle of something. Are you okay?" Clay's voice was careful.

"Now that I know you're safe, yes. Just…look, I can't go into details, but I'll call you before you plan to leave. Don't take a Zephyr-model plane anywhere—" I turned to look at Tawny, who looked pale with her mouth set.

"Um, sure. We can do that. I'm kind of freaking out about you right now. You're not acting right," Clay said.

"I'm fine."

"Do you need to talk to someone?"

"Who?" I asked, amused.

"I don't know. You've been acting kind of pissed and distract-ed for a while. I thought it was about your break-up, but—"

"That's really done. I promise I'm not fixated on that anymore."

I was glad my phone was on private. I didn't want Tawny to hear this conversation because Clay was making me feel like an idiot for being unable to let Kara go for so long.

I heard Abbi's voice, also sleepy, asking Clay who he was talking to.

"Enjoy your bride. And your honeymoon. And definitely skinny dip."

"Plan on it after our nap. You sure…"

"I'm sure. If you're good, so am I." Though, I planned to text the rest of my family to make sure they stayed out of the air until this situation was resolved.

"Cool. Catch up with you later. Love you, Colt."

"Love you, too, Clay. Give my best to Abbi."

But Clay had already hung up, no doubt more interested in Abbi than whatever I had to say.

———

I started driving again. The sooner I could get rid of this woman, the better.

"Do you know what an ethical hacker is? I mean, the point of the job?" Tawny asked, breaking the brooding silence that had fallen inside my car.

"Yeah." I'd just spent over eight years on Northwestern's campus, and that job had exploded during my tenure as a student, as had the digital security major.

Tawny tucked a strand of hair behind her ear. A pine needle floated through the air before it hit her breast and tumbled down to her lap.

"Why do you think Howie contacted you specifically?" I wasn't sure why that bothered me, but it did.

"To feel me out," she replied immediately.

"What does that mean?"

"He told me he'd heard I could be bought off."

"And why would he think that?"

She hesitated for a long minute. "It's happened before."

"Being tempted?"

But she didn't answer, which frustrated me.

Good thing we were closer to the town because I was pretty sure she'd just admitted to securities fraud or some kind of illegal shit. What was that called? The dark web, maybe. She probably worked in that, especially if she was trying to catch men involved in a big-time conspiracy to bank off aviation parts. That whole industry was well-regulated and maintained many safety protocols.

I couldn't imagine what would make people risk the lives of others...except greed.

And Tawny was mixed up with them.

She waved her hand. "We're off-topic. I think Howie hired me because he thought he could buy me off."

"And he stabbed you when you refused," I said, catching on.

Chapter 11 | Tawny | Sunday

"Yes," I whispered, looking down at my hands. I couldn't face him, not with the shame crashing through me, a personal tsunami of mortification freezing my vocal cords.

"Hemp said Howie shouldn't know where you were," Colt said.

"He shouldn't have. I have a place in Seattle. I came out here because…"

Because the case reminded me of the one I'd started with my father. The one where he died, and I'd wanted—needed—to feel closer to him. He'd bought the small space after my parents' divorce since Mom didn't want their bigger house in Montesano. She'd used the money from its sale to move to Laramie and start over.

I compressed my lips. I didn't know this man. Sure, he'd saved me, but that didn't mean our world views aligned or we were going to ride off into the sunrise together. He was probably just a good Samaritan.

Get it together, Tawny, I thought. *You've been too freaked out by this case and spending way too much time alone.*

"Hemp wanted me to meet him at a cafe in Montesano. One of the best in the area and sure to be crowded with locals," I said. "Can you drop me at that one? Hemp will meet me."

"That's a plan," he said. "I really hope they're open. I need coffee."

"Should we call in the smoke from the fire?" I asked.

Colt shook his head. "The sheriff said he'd send someone out to your place. They'll know by now. And if you're right about the location, then we need to put more space between you and whoever set that fire."

We.

Warmth blossomed in my chest. I couldn't think of a time I'd been part of a "we." But, with Colt, he wouldn't pat me on the head and go along his merry way like Hemp had at my father's funeral.

Don't look back, and be thankful for this chance, Tawn. The dark web is called that for a reason—good thing Shepard didn't pull you down into his mess far enough to keep you from a future.

I hated remembering that day. My dad, my rock, just…gone. He'd asked me to look into the guy, dig as deep as I needed, and then he was shot and killed moments later.

But Colt wouldn't leave me. He wouldn't… *Wait.* I didn't know that. This guy was affecting my decision-making skills. I couldn't let that happen. I knew what happened when I trusted the wrong person. I knew what it was like to face the consequences—big, bad ones—alone. I shivered, remembered the cuffs around my wrists, the hard chair causing my back and rump to ache.

The police detective left me there, for hours. Just waiting for me to crack and spill my guts. I bit back a whimper, shoving down the memory.

Focus, Tawny.

Make sure that data is uploaded and get to the FBI, where you belong.

That was my mission, what I needed to do. Not worry about Colt or how handsome he was or how his eyes made my insides sing and melt all at once.

Where had that thought come from? I'd noticed *his eyes*? No, I had a love affair with his eyes.

I pressed my palm flat against my good thigh, my other arm cradling my laptop. Colt was nice and all. He'd probably saved my life, and for that I owed him both a favor and to leave him alone as soon as possible.

I nodded to myself. Smart. Clean. I had no time for romantic entanglements. Not while I was working for the FBI. And I couldn't refuse to work for them until I finished this project.

A project that might well cost me my life. At least if Howie and his buddies got their way.

Chapter 12 | Colt | Sunday

Today wasn't going as I'd expected. At all.

Tawny wasn't what I'd expected, either. Not for an ethical hacker. She was clearly smart, which I expected based on our conversations. She seemed quiet and shy, which was another potential stereotype of a computer geek. Also, independent and tough, which didn't altogether fit her pixie exterior.

The woods thinned as we headed down Hwy 101, bringing us back to civilization. If you could call Montesano, a town of roughly three thousand residents, civilization. More importantly, the place where I got to part ways with my vexing, fascinating, and way too interesting car mate.

I hoped taking Tawny with me would prove smart. So far, I couldn't say my decision making—since I'd started dating Kara, I'd guess—had been all that stellar.

"I'm not sure you'll get an ISP connection."

"Let me worry about that," she said.

"You have a way to hack into the cellular network," I said with a sigh.

She glanced over, her brows tight over her nose. "What do you know about hotspots and cell towers?"

"Enough to know that other people can track them, too," I said.

"Possibly. But I'll mask my location and encrypt any of the data that could give someone my identity. Standard procedure," she said with a wave of her hand.

Standard procedure my ass.

"Look, this isn't normal—"

"We agree on that—"

"And what you're talking about is pretty high-level techie stuff—"

"High-level techie, at your service," she said with a triumphant grin.

Well, at least she appeared to be feeling better, but now, I wasn't.

"This is spy stuff," I said. "You get that—what you're doing, what you're talking about—it's, like, Bond."

"Yeah, it's a kind of espionage. Corporate, if you will. Sanctioned by the US government. I have the wire transfers to prove it." She shook her head and her lips compressed in a firm line—

And…time to focus on the road.

"So, what happens then?"

"I go to Seattle. Hang out at some offices until the right people are in custody."

"And you'll need to get your wound taken care of," I said. She hadn't mentioned it, and that worried me. There were all types of infections that could cause fever or gangrene or…

"After," she said.

"What?"

"After this operation is over, I can get medical attention," she said.

"Tawny," I said. Then, I sighed. What could I say?

"Look, I get this is crazy—that involving you is crazy. But, on the plus side, you know your brother and his wife are safe and will remain so. Added bonus: you can be free of me in…" She squinted, thinking. "Like, three minutes."

"It's not like the last hour has gone swimmingly for me, either," I said.

She snorted. "I'm the one who was stabbed. And then I was picked up by a guy dressed like Jason from that slasher movie, minus the mask. On top of all that, I'm pretty sure my father's cabin, which held all of his possessions, burned to the ground."

"Touché."

"Do you have any water?" she asked. "I'm lightheaded."

I pulled a large stainless-steel bottle from my door pocket. "Sorry. I should have thought to offer this to you before. Here."

She grabbed the bottle and uncapped it. She drank deeply, sighed, then drank again.

"Want some?" she asked.

I shook my head, though I knew I should take her up on the offer. On the other hand, I'd made my own bed to lie in and Tawny hadn't. For that reason alone, she deserved the water. I could survive another few minutes of the pounding in my skull. I hoped.

"I really need that cup of coffee. Or the entire pot."

Tawny shot me a look, her amber eyes filled with concern. My fatigue and worry laid like a painfully heavy burden on my shoulders and I wanted nothing more than to shake them off.

She straightened up, her eyes flaring open just a little. Yes, I should have been watching the road, but I liked looking at her.

Chapter 13 | Tawny | Sunday

"Tell me about your dad," Colt said.

"He was an undercover agent. He died during an assignment—just like I always feared he would."

"So, he was in with the FBI?"

I hesitated. "I'm not sure."

Colt shot me a scowl. "I got the sense you were close. How could you not know?"

"Because, apparently, there was an awful lot about him I didn't know. I can tell you that when he died, he worked for the county as a deputy sheriff."

Colt continued to frown. "They do undercover work?"

"Some. For the kind of opioids that were—probably still are—on the peninsula? Yeah."

Colt kept his gaze on the road. "I'm sorry about your dad."

"Thanks."

I studied Colt from the corner of my eye. He looked sickly, as if he suffered from nausea or a hangover. His stomach growled louder and angrier than before. I couldn't remember the last time I put food in my system, and my own belly began to gurgle back in sympathy.

He drove with ease, his wrist slung over the wheel, showcasing his watch. His expensive, made from precious materials watch with a brand name I'd never actually witnessed before in person.

Based on the watch, the brand-new vehicle—noted by the smell and the less-than-two-thousand miles on the odometer—I'd decided the man must be well-off. Like, *really*.

That meant Colt was way out of my league. For many reasons, not least of which my background. It would never mesh with Colt's. And, anyway, he was about to drop me off at the Beehive. I glanced out the window, trying to ascertain our location based on the terrain.

I'd never been a huge fan of the crowds that flocked to Montesano, so I wasn't familiar with the food options.

"I'm sorry for messing up your trip." I wondered if he was angry with me since he'd gotten stuck babysitting me until I could get to Hemp.

Well, for the moment, anyway. I wondered why I cared about this stranger so much. Soon, we'd part ways. And if I followed through on the plans I'd been building, I'd soon be moving to Wyoming to be closer to my mother.

A soft glow warmed my chest. My mom, a former social worker, had left my father when he started his undercover work, claiming it wasn't safe for me. And she was right.

I'd disappointed her when I moved in with my dad during what should have been my high school years, choosing to have my father "homeschool" me, which meant I taught myself since my dad was rarely around. That wasn't the last painful rift in my relationship with Mom, but it had proven to be the one that caused us to splinter seemingly too far apart to correct course.

After years of tentative communication, we'd come to a

healthier place. When she took in two kids from the system, I'd started sending her money to support her growing crowd, proud of her decision to help needy kids. But any ambition to expand her foster care abilities was on hold until she sorted out her parents' health situation.

She needed my help, and I was finally in a position to offer it. Or would be, in a few short months. Thanks to my job with the FBI and the freelance clients I'd cultivated in the last couple of years, I managed to pay off the last of my student debts—six years at Stanford hadn't fit into a social worker's and a sheriff deputy's budget, no matter how good my grades. I had been lucky to get some scholarships, too, but my living expenses were still much higher than they would have been if I'd stayed in Washington.

Now, I had built a nice nest egg, thanks to working insane hours that left little time for socializing or spending the money I'd managed to amass.

I wasn't going to miss the FBI's cases, though. Especially not after this current one.

I'm going to kill you, Tawny.

Howie's words echoed through my head. I shuddered hard as if trying to erase the image, and the sound of Howie's voice, from my body and mind.

The town's first buildings appeared, and I sighed with relief.

"Uh…" Colt glanced up at the rearview mirror. "We've got company."

A large blue car zipped around us on the highway, ignoring all speed limits. A moment later, a boxy old cruiser pulled onto the highway, lights and sirens flickering to life.

I sat still, a deep cold penetrating my body.

"Um…"

"What?" Colt asked.

I cleared my throat. "That was my car."

Chapter 14 | Colt | Sunday

My gaze shot up to the passing car, noting its dated body style before I returned my attention to the road.

"That *asshole*. He stole my car."

She tightened her arm around her laptop and slammed her fist against her uninjured thigh.

I didn't need more proof. I was definitely Team Tawny in this crazy scenario I'd managed to drop into.

"I'm sorry I doubted you," I said.

I turned into the parking lot of the Beehive, circling toward the back of the building. As I pulled into the space, a lithe woman in a dark coat slid into a silver Mercedes SUV. For a moment, she faced me, and I grunted.

"What?" Tawny asked.

I shook my head. "Never mind. Just seeing things."

Tawny's eyes were intelligent and assessing, not unlike many of the professors I'd worked with over the years, as she studied me. She made a disapproving sound in the back of her throat.

My phone rang, startling me out of reverie. "Hello?" I asked.

"Colten. Sheriff Hemp Sullivan. Change in plans. You need to get Tawny out of town. Pronto."

"All right," I said. "I can do that, I guess. But, erm, why?"

"Caught a suspect in Tawny's car."

"We saw him zip by," Tawny said. "Any idea who he is?"

"No time for details now. Keep your phone on. I'll call soon as I'm able." He hesitated. "Tawny, Nick Fowler's involved. And from what Russo said, he isn't happy."

Tawny sucked in a long, harsh breath as the little color in her face drained. I guessed she knew the guy—and I wasn't going to like what I learned about him.

Chapter 15 | Tawny | Sunday

I closed my eyes and dropped my forehead to my knees. Nick Fowler.

That was a name I'd never wanted to hear again.

"Hey. Are you okay?" Colt asked.

No. I was *not* okay. "Sure."

"Can you tell me what's going on? Who's this Fowler guy? Why did the sheriff just ask me to take you…never mind. Sounds like they caught the person in your car, so that's good."

I didn't even bother to nod. Colt cast one longing look at the diner but pulled out of the lot.

I managed to sit up. A silver SUV pulled out behind us—the same car that Colt had looked at in the lot.

"Is *that* car following us?"

I studied it, surprised when the driver switched on the high beams. I squinted against the additional glare.

He glanced up into the rearview mirror for a brief moment. His lips compressed into a flat, hard line. "I guess we're going to find out."

He sped up so that the scenery flashed by too fast for me to make out individual trees or streets, let alone houses. The silver vehicle followed, creeping closer as we edged out of town. Trees blurred into a continual slash of green.

I glanced out the side mirror. "Colt," I said, my voice taking on a note of concern. "That car's getting really close."

"I see that," he said.

His knuckles were white against the steering wheel, and his face a tense mask of concentration. His gaze whipped to the right, the left, up ahead, into the mirror.

"Hold on."

I grabbed the handle tucked next to the window and squeezed. Colt lifted his foot off the gas and slammed it onto the brake. The tires screamed as the brake pads fought the momentum.

The car behind us clipped our back bumper, sending us to the right—directly toward that row of green trees.

The car behind us wasn't as lucky. I heard the crunch of metal and the squeal of tires. Colt yanked the wheel to the left, practically standing on the brake. We shuddered to a halt. A tree was so close to my window I could see each individual section of bark.

"Oh my…" Words failed me.

"That was too close," he muttered. "Too fucking close."

He looked behind him, a pained expression on his face. I glanced back, too, shocked to find only an empty road behind us.

"Where'd it go?" I asked.

"Not sure," Colt said.

"And I really don't want to find out."

He shoved the car into reverse, his hand much steadier than mine. He inched back, maneuvering carefully until he could straighten out and start driving again.

"We need to call Hemp with this information," I said, already pressing the button to the recent-calls list to find his number.

"I think," he said, his voice quavering slightly. "That you're going to have to tell me who Nick Fowler is...and what the fuck I agreed to in taking you to my cabin."

Chapter 16 | Colt | Sunday

She blew out a breath when she rang off with Hemp after telling him about our most recent incident.

"Maybe he'll find the woman," Tawny said.

I bit my cheek, wondering if I should have mentioned how much the woman who pursued us looked like Kara.

I shook my head. I must have been mistaken. There was no reason for her to be out here.

"I'm sorry this happened, Colt," she said, her voice small, pulling me out of my head. "You're right—I owe you the truth. Even if it is ugly. And painful."

"This doesn't sound like a fairy tale."

"Because it's not. Nick Fowler works for an agency called R.I.S.K. Associates."

"Never heard of it."

"That's because you're an honest, law-abiding citizen."

I frowned. "I'm not liking where this is going."

"And I'm not liking sharing this story."

She huffed out a breath that sounded somewhere between a laugh and a sob. "When I was working on my master's, I started freelancing... I thought if I had more money, then my dad would quit doing undercover work. He'd told me that he wouldn't let me pay for my education—that was his responsibility. But, a white-hat hacker makes a pretty good income. I planned to start in the field after my bachelor's but…" She shook her head. "Off topic."

"But what?"

"Stanford wanted me. I was flattered. I accepted their grad-school package. The tuition was covered, but not room and board. The Bay area's expensive, and my dad wanted me to focus on my studies. He kept sending me money, so I started wiring it back. I didn't see him for weeks at a time. The last time I saw him, whatever he was doing, it was…scary, bad. He looked done in."

My stomach iced over. "I'm getting the sense that didn't really work out?"

She shrugged but the movement was weak, her expression filled with despair.

"He came to my place, asked for my help. Of course I agreed. I didn't understand then…"

Ah, hell. "*Your father* got you involved in something shady?"

She flinched. "I don't…I don't know what his plan was. He died; shot as he left my place. I was so scared…"

She ran her hands over the laptop's case. I bet she was. Her father asked for her help and then he died. That didn't inspire warm, fuzzy feelings.

"When the police showed up, they took me down to the station. I was taken to a room and handcuffed to the chair. A detective questioned me, but during that period, another man walked in. He was big, and his *eyes*…" She shuddered.

"I was freaked out that the police learned what my dad asked me to do, and I'd be on academic probation, lose my certification. Never work in the field."

I nodded. I didn't know any other ethical hackers, but there was an ingrained bias against the group—most industry personnel seemed to think there was no such thing as a good hacker, and Tawny's story would reinforce those stereotypes.

"Something changed," I said, "if you're still working in the field."

She *should* have stayed on the right side of the law, no matter what her dad asked of her. Then there wouldn't be a cloud of doubt hanging over her now. But…I thought of my dad's affairs. Would I have had the balls to call him out on them, knowing what I knew now? How much he'd hurt and embarrassed my mom?

Would I have wanted to rock the boat in the first place? I'd wondered if I'd seen the signs and subconsciously ignored them, not wanting to admit there was a problem. So…did that really make me better than Tawny? No. I needed to admit that I'd hidden behind my insecurities, let my fears overtake me.

She'd admitted her mistakes. That was brave. Really fucking brave—especially in her line of work.

This woman, this gorgeous woman, was turning my every preconceived notion on its head…and I liked her *more* for the disruption.

"What does this have to do with the guy?"

"Nick Fowler."

Each time she said his name, a slight chill seemed to creep down her spine like the man was worse than any monster under the bed. I didn't like the way she spoke of him—or the power he seemed to have over her psyche.

"He sat down at the table after handing the detective his card.

The detective left me there with Nick. He was so…cold. Assessing."

He didn't sound like a guy I'd want to meet…under a bed or anywhere else. Her stark features, and the way she hugged herself, had me second-guessing my request for information.

"He said I better not ever dig into the part of the web my dad wanted me to penetrate."

"The dark web."

She nodded.

"He knew all about that conversation. I don't know how, but he knew everything."

That made my skin sizzle with goose pimples.

"Nick told me if I followed his advice, he'd get me a job with the FBI," she said, her tone soft. "And he'd make sure my dad's reputation remained clear. It was all I had left of him…"

Anger burned in my throat. This Fowler dude sounded stone-cold. He'd pressed hard into Tawny's love and loyalty. I couldn't fault her for wanting to help her father. Fuck, no. I'd want to do the same thing.

This girl. Her story. The cynic in me wanted to reject her tale. It was far-fetched. But I'd seen her terror at his name, and I'd been run off the road. I'd found her in a heap, bleeding and cold.

So far, her story might be the only full truth I'd gotten today.

She paused. Her gaze cut to my face. I turned to meet it for a brief moment. She looked so small, so scared. So tired. I wasn't sure how long she'd been working with the FBI, but the service wore her out.

I hated her defeated expression.

"I started that weekend."

"Working for the FBI?"

She nodded. "Agent Russo was my handler then. She's the one who recruited me from Stanford. Well, Nick put me on her team. When she moved to Seattle, she had me come with her."

Her brief pause told me she suspected something.

"Come on, Tawny. Finish this."

She plucked at the make-shift bandage on her leg.

"I think my father worked with Fowler's group on some of his undercover assignments. I think the one…when my father died, it had to do with Nick. He never came out and said that, but I'm pretty sure I'm right because there was no other reason I've ever been able to think of for him to get me involved with the FBI. He could have let me dig into that case, into the dark web. I'm pretty sure I would have."

"But you never did?"

She shook her head. "My father hadn't given me anything in writing, but when I returned to my apartment, I knew someone had been there and searched it." Her shoulders sagged. "I found a program on my machine—one that was designed to notify Nick Fowler if I entered any of the dark web pages."

That sounded ominous as fuck.

"I hadn't done any of that—not until I came out here. I was… I couldn't find anything on Howie before four years ago. He just sort of…appeared into the world. I thought if I checked into the dark web, I might learn more about him. He showed up before I got very far, but I did find that connection between Shasta and Zephyr, which isn't anywhere on either company's servers."

I'd expected her to have gone black-hat—rogue, bad, whatever the layman term was. Then, now. She had the skill set, and she had reason not to trust the investigative forces, reasons to turn against them. But she hadn't—not until she was forced into it by circumstances.

Tawny turned to face me; eyes filled with tears. "Howie must have had people watching. He found me so quickly, and now you're involved. I'm so sorry, Colt. I can't tell you how sorry I am that you found me on the side of the road. If you want to leave me here, I understand."

"I'm not leaving you on the side of the road."

No way. Tawny might not be the sweet, innocent girl I'd first pegged her as—or she might be. I wasn't sure anymore. Her story was crazy—convoluted. But one thing I was very sure of: I liked her. She was smart, resilient. And trying her best to protect me.

So, I'd do the same for her.

Chapter 17 | Tawny | Sunday

"The cabin has good security. We're safer there than out here," Colt said.

"Where's there?"

"On the lake."

So, another hour north of Montesano—further from Seattle. Prickles of annoyance danced over my nape. "I'm sure that's why Nick Fowler wants me there."

"You think he looked me up?"

"I know he did. Nick is…something else. He has all these resources. Agent Russo, Hemp, they all respect him, maybe even fear him. He wants me with you, for some reason."

"Well, aren't I flattered."

My lips compressed. "Seriously. You can just drop me on the side of the road. If Nick's got someone coming for me…"

Colt glanced over, checking in on me as if he knew I'd resigned myself to a terrible fate.

"Don't do that. I might not have unlimited resources like R.I.S.K., but I have a lot. And I'll use them as best I can to help you."

"You don't have to do that," I said.

"I do." He shifted on his seat. "If I'm right about who tried to run us off the road, then…well, there's no point in me running or hiding anyway."

That sounded ominous.

"Who do you think it was?"

He continued to drive for a few more miles. "Kara," he said.

"Kara? Should I know someone named Kara?" I asked.

He shrugged.

"But you know her?"

"She's my ex."

Oh. Well, that might explain her running him off the road. Maybe she was jealous and couldn't stand the idea of him being with another woman. Oh, crap. In this scenario, *I* would be the other woman.

"How much further?" I asked.

"About twenty miles. Tell me about your FBI gig."

"Well."

I tucked a strand of hair behind my ear.

"I help take down some of the worst white-collar criminals in the country. I've worked with Agent Russo on twenty-four cases. My favorite was the man we caught last year."

"What did he do?"

"He had a bunch of shell companies that laundered money from his illegal arms-trading."

"And you found that out on the white side of the web?" Colt asked.

"Yep. He thought he'd buried the business deep enough, but I linked all the companies, and now he's in prison."

Colt's jaw clenched. "I had no idea the world was this messed up."

"It's pretty horrible. At least, that's what I see."

I was quiet.

"The fact that Nick is himself involved tells me just how bad this situation is. I knew he'd be mad about me breaching the dark web, but I had to when I found the connections between the parts and the…never mind. That's not integral to our conversation. The bottom line is I found out that Howie has exploited the companies he's bought before, basically turning them from legitimate manufacturers into shells that he can exploit. I had no idea that me following Howie's trail would make Nick mad enough to come after me. I'm so sorry I involved you," I said again.

"I'm not," he said.

"What?"

I turned toward him, mouth gaping. How could he be anything but annoyed?

He chuckled.

Colt grimaced. "Kara? She dumped me for Howie."

Oh, well, then maybe she wasn't crazy. Maybe she was part of Howie's inner circle.

"Why didn't you say something to Hemp?"

He shot me a glance. "Because I could have been wrong. And she's supposedly married to Howie as of today, so if I'm wrong, and I accuse her of something—"

"You look like a jealous ex," I finished for him.

Colt nodded.

"That dirty dog," I exclaimed. "He's married to her? He said something about breaking up with a woman. Yes…he *did* mention that name. Kara. What does she gain by driving us off the road?"

"Not sure," Colt replied. "But I think we need to find out."

My mind was on the fact that Howie Novak shouldn't—didn't exist, and his link to Kara was worrisome. And that she'd tried to drive us off the road, more so.

Once again, the car was silent. But it was a comfortable silence. I began to relax—the first time I'd done so since I'd let Howie into my cabin. Everything ached and my leg throbbed, but I felt…safe.

That was a strange sensation, something I hadn't felt since before my father died.

"I wouldn't have known to keep my family off private jets. Finding you might well have saved someone I love. I can't ever be sorry about that."

Fair enough.

"I still don't like that you're in danger."

"Gotta toss that back at you, Tawn."

I wrinkled my nose at his use of Hemp's nickname for me but didn't bother to correct him.

"So, something's bothering me."

"Just one thing?" I asked.

"Smartass." He smiled, taking the sting from his words.

"How did that guy—the one your dad wanted you to look into—?"

I frowned. "Yeah?"

"Could this Nick Fowler dude have set you up?"

I nibbled my lip, considering. "You mean that my dad was working for him, but Nick really wanted me?"

"Yeah, maybe. Or…"

Dread swirled in my gut. "Or what?"

"Or...I don't want to say it."

I swallowed hard. "Nick shot my dad because he was looking into something he didn't like and pretty much strong-armed me into not following up on the dark web?"

Colt's jaw worked and his eyes darkened. With displeasure? I didn't know him well enough to be sure. "Something to consider."

"That's sinister, but, yes, I've considered it. Just like I also considered that Nick might have pulled me in to protect me." I shook my head. "I don't know. I don't know who killed my father or why. But I do know that when I get out of my deal with Nick Fowler, I plan to find out."

"I can't blame you for wanting to know. But...if any of our hypotheses prove correct, you might be in danger when you go digging."

"That's a risk I'm willing to take," I said.

———

Colt pressed a code on the large metal gate and pulled into the drive of a sprawling wood-and-glass home that really did not meet my standard for "cabin." While I gawked, he continued driving along the graveled drive that led behind the home to the five-car garage that swung out in its own large wing behind the rest of the structure. He picked up his phone and must have used some app to open one of the garage bays. The wooden, carriage-style doors slid open and Colt pulled into the bright space. The floor was white, without a single tire mark.

"We do not have the same vocabulary," I muttered.

"What?"

"This is *not* a cabin. My three-room, twelve-hundred-square-foot rustic box is—was—a cabin. *This* is a pleasure palace."

Colt snorted. "Not quite. And it better never become one. I'd have to beat up some people."

"Whatever. It's huge."

"There are normally five to fifteen people staying here at a time."

I continued to stare as I climbed out of the vehicle, so intoxicated with my surroundings I barely noticed my sore leg.

Colt grabbed his bag and slid out another canvas bag loaded with groceries. I reached for the groceries and he let me take them. After closing his SUV's hatchback with a push of a button, he led us through a spacious mudroom that doubled as an airy laundry room, and into the kitchen, which was probably bigger than my entire cabin.

The cabinets were alder, and the countertops were a bluish-gray engineered stone, which surprised me. I assumed a higher-end material like granite or marble. The floor was slate, a popular choice in these parts. I'd never seen a range like the one that dominated one wall.

"Colt, this place is like stepping into a magazine spread. In fact, I'm not sure some of the places in those spreads are this nice. Your family isn't just rich, they're *rich*," I said.

"And this is why I may never have another relationship," he said.

I turned toward him, setting the bag on the counter, my laptop next to it. Though, I wouldn't go far without the machine.

"Huh?"

He shook his head, but his eyes were stormy, and his mouth twisted in an unhappy grimace.

I blinked as understanding slowly hit my foggy brain.

"You get hit on a lot, don't you? Because of your wealth?"

"It's not *my* money. My father's...well, he's done well. He's part of a well-known rock band."

"Huh. You're the first famous person I've ever met."

"I'm not famous," he said, looking affronted, maybe even slightly freaked out.

"You kind of are," I said.

Colt waved his hand. "Nope."

"Well, whatever. Must be nice to have a rich, famous family. And for the record, I make a pretty good income myself."

Colt raised his eyebrow, a small smile quirking the edges of his lips. "So, you don't want me for my bank account?"

I started to giggle. "Believe me, your bank account wasn't part of my calculations when we were almost smashed into a tree. I was much, much more impressed with your skill under pressure and ability to keep us from crashing. Also, you're a good medic. Those traits matter more to me than any of this." I waved my hand around to indicate our luxurious surroundings.

He cracked a smile. "Thanks. I needed to hear that."

I returned his grin. "My pleasure. But, seriously, you have to know you're a great guy."

His expression dimmed.

"My ex didn't consider me much of a catch."

"Yeah, well, if you're talking about Kara, she had a thing for a guy who steals money and hurts people. Her opinion of you might just raise my opinion of you."

This time his smile warmed all the way to his eyes, but he seemed almost bashful. "You do know just what to say."

I snorted. "Computer geek." I pointed at my chest. "I'm better with machines and code than people."

My quip fell flat, mainly because I really wanted to be good at communicating with Colt. But this—our banter—was new to me. I wasn't sure I was doing it right, and I knew he wouldn't be there with me if he hadn't been kind enough to stop and help me.

"Let's get these groceries put away. Then, maybe you'd like a shower and a bed."

"That sounds amazing."

After we added the fresh foods to the fridge and he showed me the well-stocked pantry, Colt led me down the hall to a well-appointed room with a queen four-poster bed, surrounded by romantic, gauzy curtains in the same bright teal of the silk comforter.

"There's a divan at the end of the bed. In matching fabric," I breathed.

"Is that what that thing is called? I always thought it was some kind of weird couch."

He shrugged. He slid his hands into his jean pockets, and I tried not to notice his biceps. Clark Kent wasn't as built as this guy. Might not be as nice either.

Yep. I liked Colten Rippey. *Really* liked him.

"My mother likes guests to be comfortable," he said.

I turned away, unable to face him. My face must reflect my dreamy covetousness. I cleared my throat in an effort to regain control over my surging passion.

"You don't understand. I adore divans."

His face scrunched in an adorable way. "Well, knock yourself out adoring."

He turned to leave. Shit. I needed something from him.

"Um…Colt?" I asked.

He turned back at the door, his bag in his hand.

"Is there any…is it possible to get some clean clothes? And a few basic tools?"

Colt's eyes softened. "I should have thought of that. I'll bring you some stuff after I put my bag in my room."

He stepped out and I settled on the edge of the divan, ignoring my impulse to lay back. My hair sifted out dust and leaves each time I turned my head and the rest of me was crusted with dirt.

Colt strode back into the room with a tall pile of clothing. He set it on the bed and turned away. On top was a small wooden toolbox.

"If you need more tools, I can go look in the garage. I gave up on the coffee. I'm beat. I think I'm going to grab a few hours of sleep. See you later, Tawny."

"Is there an office?" I asked.

"Yeah. Other side of the dining room, by the front door."

"Okay. Mind if I use it?" I asked.

"Whatever you need," he said. He turned and headed back toward his room.

I tried to ignore the bereft feeling in my belly. But what did I expect? This man had been saddled with me and my insane set of problems. Swallowing down my unhappiness, I opened my laptop.

And stared at the blank, cracked screen.

I squinted. Okay. There was a bit of battery life left though I couldn't read how much. I entered my password. The hard drive seemed intact, which was very lucky. I keystroked into my email, surprised when the program loaded.

Damn. The message hadn't sent.

I tried to resend, but the email lagged in the outbox.

I took my computer back down the hall and sat in front of the router, using up precious battery life in an effort to amp up the network. I opened another screen and slipped back into Shasta Aeronautic's backdoor. My eyes ached from squinting, but the cracks made it hard to read the code.

I hesitated and went back to the email. Seventy-nine percent. Crap. I needed that to go through.

I broke it into smaller bits, along with a note to Russo that I was at a safe house of Nick Fowler's choosing. Because he was Nick Fowler, he'd know where I was and extract me when he was ready.

Then, I clicked back to the other screen. My fingers flew over the keys as I built out a time bomb.

I wanted to destroy the possibility of future sales between Shasta and its customers, which meant I had to take out the database for the faulty parts even as I transferred all profit and loss information to my secure server. I set the predetermined time for six hours.

That completed, I hesitated, fingers hovering over the keys. Blowing out a breath, I built a trojan program, adding Kara to the list of keywords. Once triggered, I would receive all emails into an account I'd set up for this purpose. I didn't like Trojan horses, but considering that Colt thought Kara tried to run us off the road, and my cabin was now probably a pile of ash, I didn't feel as bad about the use of a malicious program that would copy over any data with the keywords I'd requested once anyone on the server opened my program on a machine within the network.

I clicked the final code and uploaded it, holding my breath in hopes my fingers hadn't failed me with a misplaced keystroke. I noted the red battery icon though I couldn't read the number next to it, thanks to one of the cracks.

The screen showed I'd uploaded the program. Good. That was two items. I clicked back to the email and grinned. *Success.*

The screen flickered black.

Okay, well, I'd managed what I needed to do. For now, anyway.

The battery died, and I didn't have a charging cable. Time to remove the hard drive. I collected the toolbox and selected the correct Phillips head. Once I removed the casing, I removed the innards and then took a flat head over the rest, scoring the wires and metal plating. I didn't want any chance of someone else getting the data. I reattached the computer's back and left it on the desk.

Checking the hard drive, I noted the bent connections. Damn. That must have happened when I smacked Howie with it or when I dropped it out the window. Hopefully, the code I'd written hadn't been compromised by the parts. No way to tell now.

I heaved a sigh of deep frustration. Could nothing go right today?

No, that wasn't a fair assessment of the situation. I was safe. I was about to be clean, and I had fresh clothes. Plus, I'd sat on an actual divan.

My smile lasted until I headed back down the hall and stood under the hot spray from the four different shower heads exploding from the wall and ceiling of the bathroom off the bedroom Colt offered me.

I cursed and cried at the pain in my leg when the water hit the cut, but I forced myself to stay still so that the water and soap would help clean the wound.

Feeling equal parts better, shakier, and worse after washing my hair and body, I put on the clean underwear Colt pilfered from somewhere and my bra—he hadn't brought one that would fit me, which I put back on because I was in a house with a man I didn't really know, with people chasing us. I wanted to just crawl in bed but decided to just get dressed again, just in case.

I rummaged through the cabinets until I found a well-stocked first-aid kit. I slathered antibiotic cream on the gash and then affixed a sterile piece of gauze with tape. My leg trembled with weariness and pain as I limped to the bedroom.

I grabbed the hard drive and tucked it under my pillow. I was asleep before the comforter and sheet settled over my body.

Chapter 18 | Colt | Monday

The screaming woke me.

Wait, not screaming.

An alarm.

The house alarm.

I bolted out of bed, adrenaline rushing through my system, as my brain fixated on Tawny.

She was in danger.

I burst out of my room and down the dark hallway. I threw open the door to her room. She wasn't there.

Breathing hard, I darted toward the main area of the house. I wasn't sure if someone else was here, so I didn't want to enter the code to turn off the alarms until I was certain we were safe.

We weren't. Rather, Tawny wasn't.

Through the doors that led to the large deck off the back of the house, I took in the scene: a man held Tawny by her arm and tears poured down her cheeks. She wore jeans and a T-shirt I'd given her from my raid on my mother's and sister's closets, along with a pair of Cassidy's hiking boots she must have discovered herself. Though the darkness made it more difficult, I gauged the distance, trying to calculate the physics in my head. The man stepped to the right, closer to the doors.

"Gotcha, jackass."

I flung the door open, using all my force to slam the door into his side. The man grunted and slid off-kilter. I slammed the edge of my palm against his wrist, breaking his hold on Tawny. She made a gurgling sound as she stumbled, but I caught her, pulling her to my chest as I hauled her back into the house and slammed the French door shut. I locked it and tugged Tawny down the hall, breathing hard.

"Colt?"

Her voice was weird—full of tears but also high-pitched. Like she was scared.

"I'll get you to safety, I promise. He won't touch you again."

"I need to talk to him."

"What? Why? He was hurting you."

"That's Hemp. The sheriff."

I stopped walking. I dropped my chin to my chest. I cursed.

"Yeah. I agree. I don't want him here, and I definitely don't want him mad at you. Could you, maybe, turn off the alarm?"

I stalked over to the wall and entered the code.

She dropped her gaze, a rosy blush staining her cheeks and neck. "And, erm, maybe you could…ah…put on some clothes?" She glanced at me, licked her lips and tipped her head aside, her face flaming.

I sighed, running my hands through my hair, trying to wake up, hating the residual blaring in my ears. And, maybe most importantly, trying to overcome the adrenaline currently pumping through my body.

"Why were you out there? How did you know he was there?"

"I didn't. I found a spider…" She trailed off. Her gaze came up to mine, dropped down to my boxer-briefs, and shot back up to my face. Her pupils were more dilated, her lips slightly parted.

She liked what she saw. I had to resist the urge to flex. Showing off for Tawny right now wasn't in the cards. We had to deal with the sheriff I'd just accosted. But after I heard more from her—her voice was huskier, thanks to her desire and it was the best aphrodisiac.

"You let a spider outside?"

"It was in the bathroom—when I got up to go pee," she said.

Oh my...she was fucking adorable. She saved a spider. And scared the ever-loving hell out of me.

"And Hemp was there. I was telling him I'd sent a message to Russo earlier and he said he'd shown up to make sure we were okay."

I shook my head and my mouth wobbled, unsure if my lips wanted to smile or frown. She stood frozen about a foot down the hallway that led to our rooms, her gaze still downcast.

"I'll field the call from the alarm company," I said.

She mumbled a reply. I caught the words *Clark Kent* and *sexy*. Considering her gaze once again skimmed my torso as she did so, and her cheeks flushed hotter, I decided I better put on some clothes.

Not for Tawny's sake—for my own.

Chapter 19 | Tawny | Monday

I couldn't drag my gaze from the long lines of his thighs, taut abdomen, and firm butt. He looked better than any of the men who had played the most recent Superman—and I loved me some Henry Cavill. My cheeks burned.

"I'll just go get dressed," he said, appearing a little sheepish. "Wait for me before you open the door."

I swallowed. "Okay."

He trotted down the hall and I bit back a moan. I leaned against the wall and let my head thud against it. I closed my eyes, remembering Colt coming to my defense like that. I managed not to fan myself, but it was a challenge. His eyes had flashed, and his face was set. He'd looked so determined.

Apparently, some part of my psyche found the idea of being a man's damsel biologically pleasing. Like, *really*.

I pressed my thighs together, trying to reduce the ache there. My attraction to Colt didn't surprise me—he was kind, intelligent. All major pluses.

But he also showed a ruthless determination that reminded me of my father. That both scared me and made me respect Colt even more. He hardly knew me, and he'd just risked his life to save me—*again*.

Because us being driven off the road had been done with

deadly intent. The people involved at the aeronautics parts company clearly weren't happy I'd been tasked to expose them.

I didn't want Colt injured—or worse—because of me.

I patted the baggie with the hard drive that I'd tucked under my shirt, reassuring myself my shirt was tucked into my pants. Not the best option for safe-keeping, but then, I didn't really have a lot of great ones at the moment.

He walked back down the hall. He wore faded jeans and the beige leather hiking boots I'd seen yesterday. He smoothed his Henley down his abs. I wanted to ogle his fit torso and taut behind some more, but that would have to wait.

"Okay. Let's do this," he said.

I let him walk up to me before I joined him.

"Thank you," I said.

He raised a dark eyebrow, the question silent but obvious in his hazel eyes.

"For being so quick-thinking. For being willing to save me."

He stopped, his hand on my shoulder, causing me to pause as well. He shook his head as he brushed my hair back from my cheek.

"I barely know you and yet I have this overwhelming desire to protect you. It doesn't make sense, and I have a sister who would be all over me about my comment just then—telling me she didn't need protecting. I get that you've been doing this a long time, I get that I just pissed off the local sheriff. But, Tawny, your continued well-being matters to me."

I gripped his hand with mine and pressed a kiss to his cheek. "Whatever else comes out of this case, I'm so glad I met you."

A strange light burned in his eyes and his features softened. Before he could say anything, Hemp banged on the door.

"Will you two quit gabbing? We have some serious stuff to discuss."

This time, I took the lead, unsure if I needed to protect Colt from Hemp.

I'd missed the big, gruff man and his cloaked brown eyes. He was the man I remembered but older, grief bowing his shoulders and mingling in his voice. His hair was thinner and grayer, but his face was sharp, mouth too wide, and small ears tucked in close to his head.

I opened the door. Hemp shot Colt a narrow-eyed glare, but behind it was a look of approval. At least, I hoped it was.

"You're being moved." His gaze cut to Colt's. "Both of you."

"Why?"

"Because people are looking for you. And after what happened to your cabin, Tawn, I don't want a repeat."

I clutched my elbows. "I don't either."

"You'll sit tight in the new place and wait for Fowler to contact you. He's mobilized and heading this way."

"Not you?" I asked.

His caterpillar brows tugged together. He shook his head. "This is above my pay-grade."

I nodded. "I'm sorry I involved you in this."

He chucked my chin—the most affection he'd shown me in ages. Tears blurred my vision. "Nothing to apologize for."

"Can I talk to him?" I asked.

"You want to talk to Nick? I thought you didn't like him,"

Hemp said.

Before I could reply, Hemp held up his hand, his head tilted. Colt stiffened. The crunch of gravel under tires. Someone was coming in fast and hard.

"Hell," Hemp muttered. "We got company."

He pulled his sidearm into his meaty paw and tossed me his keys. "Remember Lulu? She's pulled off into the trees to the left, about a quarter-mile north of here. Get to her and head along Lake Quinault. Ten miles, give or take a bit. There's a turn that's barely more than a track. Take it about a mile and bear right. There's a cabin. Well, shack."

"On Pinewood?" I asked.

"Yeah. You know the place."

"But—"

"*No time*, Tawny. Just go—get out of here. It's stocked with some essentials."

I squeezed my hand around the keys and pressed a kiss to his cheek. "Thanks, Hemp." I hesitated. "And I'm sorry I didn't save my dad. And I'm so sorry I—"

He shook his head. "Get gone. Stay safe."

He called in his location and mentioned, in police lingo, a break-in in progress. He mouthed, "Go!" before he edged forward and into the front room…just as the front door smashed off its hinges.

"My computer," I said.

"Leave it," Hemp said.

"I can't." Panic clawed at me. Colt winced as gunshots reverberated through the house. We heard Hemp yelling for backup, that shots had been fired.

Colt dragged me into the laundry room on the other side of the kitchen and threw open the window. He kicked out the screen. It clattered onto the deck below. I gritted my teeth. *Again.* For the second time, I was going to fall out a window in an effort to save myself from bodily harm.

Colt slid out with way more grace than I ever had. He turned and motioned me forward. Footsteps sped down the hallway toward us. I launched myself into the gap. The concussive sound of bullets was closer, causing my heart to pound. I hit the ground with a bone-jarring thud. Already, Colt was tugging me forward, crouching low like some kind of professional cop. We moved with as much speed as my shorter, hurt legs allowed. I heard a few loud, percussive pops as we reached the tree line just before the tree bark exploded near our heads. We both lifted our arms, trying to protect our faces from flying debris. Colt sprinted ahead, and I forced my legs to keep moving.

I tired quickly, and it wasn't just because of the wound. I was starving and probably dehydrated.

I promised myself that if I managed to get out of this alive, I'd take up some cardio exercise that would ensure I could outrun even Boston marathoners.

We dashed between branches and over tree roots and rocks, my breath loud and guttural, but I refused to slow even as my vision dimmed.

We burst into a clearing and there she was—Lulu, the seventies Ford pickup. Colt reached it first and I tossed him the keys. He opened the driver's door and got in. I scrambled around to the passenger side, scrambling into the cab a couple of moments later.

"Shit. Can you drive one of these things?" He pointed at the stick shift. A manual transmission. I nodded, too out of breath to speak. He'd already shoved the key into the ignition, so we climbed over each other to change places. I checked that it was in neutral, released the parking brake, and started the big truck. She roared to life as I tried to push in the clutch to shift it into gear, but the seat was too far back. I screamed a curse and felt around for the lever to move the seat closer.

After some fumbling and unable to find it, I stood up and slammed my foot onto the clutch. I felt Colt's arm slide around my waist as he slid over and brought me into his lap behind the wheel, giving me the correct depth I needed to reach the pedals. I gunned it and we clipped a tree, I winced, but I shifted into second and got us out of the tree line.

Light had breached the sky to the east, so it was almost sunrise. I blew out a breath. We'd managed a night in Colt's swanky cabin but never managed to eat any of that food. My stomach growled at the thought.

Running for my life really sucked.

We bounced onto the road, and I shifted into third, keeping my foot heavy on the gas. Once I hit fourth gear, I could almost breathe normally again.

Almost.

"You think they saw us? That they'll follow?" I asked.

Colt kept his arm around my waist, and I noted his shaking hand as he flattened it onto my stomach.

"I really don't want to find out."

Chapter 20 | Colt | Monday

Tawny tucked her hair back behind her ear, something I'd noticed she did when she was nervous or self-conscious. I was already picking up her little quirks. Somehow, that was comforting.

I couldn't see her face, but I could feel her body trembling.

"How's your leg? You didn't get hit did you?"

"I'm okay," she said.

She sounded scared but also amped up. That race out of what should have been a safe place slammed adrenaline through our bodies. We'd take a while to calm from it.

"Are you hurt?"

She started to turn toward me.

"Focus on the road," I said. "I'm fine."

She drove in silence, and I was content to hold her in my lap. In fact, she felt good there, her butt pressed into my thighs.

"Do you see a radio or some other device? Maybe a phone?"

I glanced around, bending as far over as I could to check under the seat with her in my lap. "Nope. Why?"

"I want to call Nick," she said. "I can't believe he moved us—and I can't believe those guys showed up. Who were they? It seemed…"

"Like a setup?" I asked, my voice soft because Hemp showing up just a few hours after we arrived at my place—which he would have had to look up—caused me to pause. But this man was Tawny's father's partner, and I worried how she'd feel if I questioned his loyalty.

"I'm being paranoid."

I didn't think so—she was being cautious. And smart. "I have my phone," I said. "Can you tell me who to call?"

She rattled off the digits and I dialed.

"I need to reach Nick Fowler," I said.

"Who is this?" barked a sharp, deep voice.

"This is Colt Rippey."

"Put it on speaker," Tawny said.

We were about to blow past the hunting shack Hemp wanted us to stay in.

"It's on speaker," Colt said.

"Nick, this is Tawny. Did you want us moved from Colt's place?"

"I didn't order that," Nick said slowly. My stomach dropped and I swallowed hard.

"Hemp told us to move to another cabin that's deeper into the woods. We heard shots fired at Colt's place...we're in Hemp's truck."

"Ditch it," Nick said immediately. "And don't go to the cabin."

"Then, where are we supposed to go?" Tawny asked.

Nick grunted. "Got an address?"

"A general location," Tawny said, rattling off the streets.

Nick grunted. "Give me a minute. I've got Abdul looking for another place close by."

We didn't speak but we both watched the odometer. Tawny

slowed the truck from eighty to twenty-five.

"Go to the cabin," Nick said. "And head in—take what you can. Leave the truck there. Maybe it'll buy you a few more minutes. We'll find you someplace safe," Nick said.

"Why don't you come get me now?" Tawny practically begged.

"Because I can't. I need to know if… Look, I'll call you back in five."

He hung up.

And still, we almost missed the turn. She shifted through the gears and pushed the big metal cab quicker than I would have up the incline. Trees whipped by. The road was rutted, and we bounced around, but she kept a fast, steady pace.

She gasped as the tiny structure came into view.

She pulled behind it and the truck was barely longer than the length of the building. "I thought this place burned down twenty years ago," she murmured.

"You know this place?"

"I know of it," she said. She reached toward the door handle, pressing her bottom against my groin.

Now was not the time to appreciate the soft feel of her ass.

My body didn't seem to care—or plan to listen.

"What is it?" I asked, hoping to refocus my attention. I cupped her hip because I wanted to feel her supple flesh and the flex of her muscle and tendon. A thrill shot through me. I had my hands on Tawny. And I liked them there.

"An old hunting cabin."

"What am I missing?" I asked.

She shook her head. She turned to meet my gaze, hers filled with such sadness it took my breath away.

"I have the vaguest memories of this place. Like I've been here—like it was important to my dad. I'm pretty sure it was his."

I kept my mouth shut.

She looked at me. "It must not still be because it was never mentioned in the divorce or his will. Still, I'm beginning to think there was an awful lot I didn't know about my father's life."

Chapter 21 | Colt | Monday

The sorrow dripping from her words caused me to move my hand in a soothing gesture up her side. She turned toward me, our noses touching, our lips a hair's breadth apart. She was lovely.

I hadn't noticed that before—not the depth of it, anyway. Her face was heart-shaped down to the tiny cleft in her sweet chin. I wanted to kiss that spot, flick my tongue over it. Instead, I opened the truck's door.

"Let's get what we can from inside." My tone was gruff, and she frowned.

"Did I…are you mad at me?" she asked. "I mean apart from the whole I totally screwed up your vacation, which I get. I'd be upset about that if I were you."

"No. I'm not mad." I shifted her a little and her eyes widened, the pupils overtaking more of her sherry-colored irises.

I managed to bite off the moan that wanted to escape at her obvious and frank appraisal.

"Fine. We should go." She was breathless, which made me even harder.

I pulled the forgotten keys from the ignition, put them in the back pocket of my jeans, and helped Tawny down. I climbed out after her, careful to lock the truck. She gazed around the space, troubled.

"Why wouldn't he tell me he still had this place?" she asked.

I wanted to know how her father could have gotten her mixed up in such dangerous work, but I didn't ask because I didn't want to hurt her more.

We picked our way toward the door, using stealth by tacit agreement. She tried the handle and it turned with ease. She gulped and my breathing spiked. This much adrenaline dumped into my body would cause one hell of a crash. Later.

I had to survive now, and I was thankful for the alert, primed state of my hearing and reflexes. Though dim, we could make out the square space: a small, efficient kitchen lay to our left and a couch with an end table at either side and a steamer trunk as a coffee table to our right. There were two doors beyond, both shadowy.

Tawny turned her head toward me. "You think it's safe?"

"I have no clue."

She sucked in a breath, let it out in a long slow stream, and stepped into the room. With a small yelp, she beelined to the steamer trunk and pushed open the top.

I inched forward and checked the bathroom. I was just moving into the bedroom when Tawny appeared at my side with a Glock in her hand. I gave her a questioning look.

She shrugged. "It was in the trunk. It's a weapon that I know how to use."

"But should you?" I asked, distaste causing my mouth to taste like sawdust.

"My dad always said guns were the last resort," Tawny said. "But since we know they're willing to use them, thanks to the new holes in your cabin, I kind of think we're at that point."

"I think you're right," I said. "Though I don't really like the assessment."

My stomach growled. Right. We'd gone to bed without a meal. I opened the dorm-sized fridge, expecting it to be empty. Instead, two packs of lunch meat and an additional two kinds of cheese sat there, along with mustard, a loaf of bread, a dozen bottles of water, and a quart of milk.

I sent up a silent thank you. Since Tawny was outside, walking the perimeter, I got to work making sandwiches. She came in as I plopped two pieces of bread onto a plate for her. "What do you take on your sandwich?"

"Anything you have. I'm starving."

"Mustard?"

"Yeah."

"You think we should take these to go?" she asked.

"Probably," I said.

I grabbed the second packet of lunch meat and shoved it into my hoodie's front pocket.

We took our sandwiches and grabbed some bottles of water before heading back out the same door we'd entered. As we walked up the incline, Tawny winced, but she kept walking.

My phone rang, and I answered it, tucking it between my cheek and ear.

"Yeah?"

"Colt? Nick, here. There's a cabin about two miles east of you. I'll text coordinates to this number. Head there. We were on our way to collect you but got waylaid in Seattle. Tell Tawny that I received her message, and it was helpful. We'll have a team on the ground to collect you tomorrow morning. Should something go wrong, I'll text from a different number. It'll read six nine two. That means head up to the meadow five miles due north of the cabin we're re-routing you to. Got that?"

"Six nine two. Got it."

"And tell Tawny not to engage Hemp, under any circumstances. Clear?"

"Yes."

He clicked off. The phone pinged and I took in the coordinates. I relayed the details of the conversation to Tawny and she nodded. I noted she picked at her food.

"You okay?" I asked.

She shrugged.

"He was my dad's partner. I can't imagine what turned him against my father. Against me. They used to be so close..."

She sighed but kept walking.

I glanced at the gun shoved into the waistband of her too-big jeans. She held her sandwiches.

"I'm sorry you had to leave the laptop," I said.

She smiled at me. "I pulled out the hard drive," she said. "Maybe the machine will act like a decoy for a while—give us some breathing space."

For some reason, the fact that she trusted me enough to tell me she'd pulled apart the laptop caused my heart to patter harder. I knew how important this machine was to her—to this case that had just proven her father's partner was willing to rat her out.

"Thanks."

We hiked on in silence.

"We quit talking after…"

"Who?" I asked.

"Hemp and I." Sadness filled her gaze.

"After your dad died?" I asked.

She grimaced. "No. After I shot Hemp."

Chapter 22 | Tawny | Monday

Colt's shocked expression would have been laughable if I weren't reliving my worst memory.

"You *shot* him?"

"I didn't know it was Hemp," I exclaimed. "I came downstairs and found my dad, bleeding out on the ground. I heard footsteps and this big, burly dude barreled toward me." I flinched, hating the memory. My stomach rolled, considering refusing the sandwich I'd inhaled. No way I could eat more now.

"I grabbed my father's gun and fired."

"His gun was with him?" Colt asked.

"Still in the holster," I said. I'd always found that odd. I wasn't sure what it meant that his weapon was still secured. Now, I had a terrible suspicion.

Colt glanced my way, his lips flattening. "You don't know he did it, Tawny."

"I don't know he didn't shoot my father either," I replied. "Not now."

"Do you have a permit for that one there?" Colt asked, waving at the pistol near my hip. He was trying to distract me. I decided to let him. Between my concerns about Hemp and my aching leg, I needed something to occupy my mind.

"I don't have to have one to have a firearm in my home, but

I do need a concealed carry to take it in any vehicle, which I do have," I told him, then frowned.

"What?"

I shook my head. "I just realized that Nick was adamant I had my permit and that I have a weapon."

"Then why didn't you use it to shoot Howie?"

"One, he was waving a knife at me, two, I didn't bring a gun with me to my dad's cabin, and three, I've seen the damage they cause all up close and personal."

I compressed my lips, thinking about my father's bloodied chest and the thick, dark pool that grew beneath him as I screamed his name, begging him to wake up—to wake *me* up from the nightmare my life had become.

"Can you shoot well? I mean, if you had to…"

I grimaced. "Maybe? As a contractor, I'm not obligated to keep my skills sharp, and I've never been a huge fan of the firing range, but I did get certified."

I'd zeroed in on Colt's distaste for the gun, but I still felt like I should ask, "Do you want a firearm?"

"I know how to fire one."

I raised an eyebrow as his face reddened.

"I used to shoot out in a field with my friends when I was an Eagle Scout. I…uh…it's physics."

"Yes, it is. So, I'd bet you're a pretty good shot," I said.

He shrugged, still eyeing my weapon.

"I grabbed this one. It's a Sig Sauer." I pulled it from inside my shirt that I'd tucked into my jeans. I'd run out of places to carry items—it wouldn't fit in my waistband with the Glock.

Colt's expression morphed into shock when I offered the pistol to him.

"It has a safety switch and a laser dot to increase accuracy. I took this one because I thought you might prefer the Sig."

He sighed. "I hope this is the only time in my life when I say I'll feel safer with the damn gun."

My heart squeezed as I took in his conflicted expression. "Me, too, Colt," I whispered.

"Hand it over," he said.

He dropped the magazine out and checked it before I could show him where it was, surprising me. I'd assumed his distaste for the weapon came from ignorance, but that clearly wasn't the case.

Colt slipped the gun into the waistband of his jeans, a look of deep concentration on his face. "Do you think Hemp will show up at the cabin soon?"

Panic bubbled in my chest. "Yes."

"So we should really up our pace, huh?"

We ate our sandwiches and drained our water bottles as we walked, and I was sweating by the time our new safe house—another hunting cabin—came into view.

It was much larger than Hemp's shack—at least I suspected it was Hemp's place. We moved forward with caution, staying off the hard-packed driveway and circling behind. We stayed in the woods for a while, observing the place. Nothing moved.

"You think it's safe?" I asked.

Colt sighed. "Who knows? But it's cold out here."

"What time do you think it is?" I asked, trying to find the sun.

"I don't know." He pulled out his phone and grimaced.

"Seven forty-five."

"Oh, well. So late."

He smirked at my sarcasm.

"We could keep walking," I said.

He shook his head. "The temperatures drop significantly as it gets dark if we have to stay out here all day, and we're not dressed properly. Our best bet is to raid the closet at least. Maybe grab some more water."

"All right. Let's go."

We broke one of the windows in a door that led into a small utility room. Ideal? No. But nothing about this situation was good. Colt closed the door and braced the knob with one of the heavy chairs from the massive, rustic solid-wood dining set. It weighed a good twenty pounds, making it a decent wedge.

We moved together through all the rooms, making sure no one was there, lurking. Our last stop was down the stairs, and I was glad to find battery packs that seemed to be related to solar energy.

"Sweet! We can shower without turning on a generator. This place is totally off the grid."

Colt nodded. "Good thing. We wouldn't want to run a generator—it would draw attention. Now…the question is how to get the pump turned on."

I watched him fiddle with some levers. "Is this design like your place?"

He shrugged. "No clue. It's just…there. Ready if we want to use it."

Once we looked over the place, we settled in the kitchen at the small oak dining table. My stomach ached from eating too quickly on top of the stress.

"Could your father have been framed?" Colt asked.

I considered Colt's question. "No clue. For as close as I thought I was with my father, it's hard for me to imagine that he would have intentionally gotten me involved in something nefarious."

My lip quivered. "He loved me, Colt. I know he did. He fought my mom for custody because she wanted to move out of state. You don't do that for a kid you don't care about."

"Come here," he said, he stood, opening his arms to me.

I got up and went to him, pressing my cheek on his chest. He slid his arms around me, and I wrapped mine around his waist.

"I think there's more going on in your story than you know."

"I think you're right." I sighed. "But right now, I'm worried about your brother and all the other people who might get hurt because I haven't been able to get Howie and his associates arrested. There's more to that situation than I've dug up so far."

"That's driving you crazy," Colt said.

I nodded.

"You don't like loose ends."

"My parents imploded when I was eleven. My mother moved to Wyoming when I was fourteen. Since their divorce, more so since she left, I like to control situations."

"So you feel safe."

"And you said your doctorate was in biology," I teased.

He tightened his hold and pressed a kiss to the top of my head. I liked that small show of affection. Probably more than I should. I sighed, snuggling closer.

"Microbiology. But what you're talking about is human

nature—something I can understand because I have my own experiences. My baby sister had Hodgkin's Lymphoma. It was…it's been hard. My parents' marriage suffered. The secure life I knew pretty much vanished."

I tipped my head back to view his eyes. "So, you managed your stress by…staying in school? A familiar environment?"

He frowned and his jaw jutted. "Maybe," he said slowly. "I hadn't thought of that. But it's possible. More, though, I got involved with a woman, mapped out our life together, and forgot to see if she was even on board."

"Kara," I said.

He smiled. "Such a smarty pants."

"She has to be involved through Howie," I said.

"Makes sense," he said. "Kara's all about wealth and power. Howie provided those things better than I ever could."

"She's a fool."

My ears burned and my cheeks flamed. I probably shouldn't have said that, but I wasn't sorry I had.

His lips quirked a little. "The bigger question is how much she knows—and why she showed up at my brother's wedding the night before Howie tried to kill you."

"What? Really?"

"Yes."

"Maybe so, you, the jilted lover, could drive to a secluded cabin in the middle of the night as opposed to getting laid by… hmmm…a bridesmaid? No…" I snapped my fingers. "Someone on the waitstaff. More anonymous."

Colt glanced over at me, a faint smile drifting over his lips.

"You read a lot of romance, Tawny?"

"Maybe," I said primly. "How do *you* know about romance?"

He laughed. "My new sister-in-law's mom is Lia Moore."

"Oh." My eyes widened. "I love her books."

"So does pretty much the rest of the population, though not everyone will admit to reading her stuff. Or watching the HBO miniseries."

"It was fantastic," I said, my voice breathy as I remembered my favorite—steamy—scenes.

"And hot," he said with a smirk.

I licked my lower lip with an exaggerated swipe of my tongue. "You thought so?"

The adrenaline from before reared up, but I wasn't interested in saving my life—I was interested in something much more life-affirming. And if the flare of heat in Colt's eyes was any indication, he felt the same way.

"Want me to show you?" he asked. The husky quality in his voice caused my thighs to clench.

"Yes."

Such a simple word.

He pulled me into the living room and onto the couch. I straddled him. His palms slid from my waist down to cup my butt, and I moaned.

And then, finally, his lips settled over mine, first in a soft brush, asking if I was okay with this. I pressed more firmly against him and parted my lips a little, letting him know I was all kinds of good with kissing. He slanted his head, his lips branding mine. Then, his tongue touched the center of my bottom lip, and

I gasped at the contact. He slid his tongue into my mouth with a deliberate stroke that reminded me all too well of what we could do together.

My hands traveled up his shoulders, over his neck, and into his hair. One of his hands gripped the back of my neck, tilting me to his preferred location, and he plundered. His shirt rubbed against mine. My nipples peaked in my sheer bra, and I moaned again. This wasn't just a kiss.

It was…

His tongue traversed the inside of my cheek, tangled with my tongue, retreated, plunged back in to learn the other side. I moaned again, loving how he learned me.

He pulled back. "Want me to stop?"

My eyes widened. His features were sharper, his gaze intent. His lips were swollen.

"No," I breathed.

His fingers flexed against my skin, a possessive gesture that I loved. My belly quivered as I pressed down, deeper into his lap— and against the impressive bulge behind his zipper.

"Don't stop," I murmured. "And for the record, you look really good almost naked."

Oh, my word. My ability to speak and embarrass myself had returned as my desire ramped up. A slow, sexy smile spread across his face.

"Did you check me out, Tawny?"

I nodded. Well, I tried, but his hand was clasped to my nape. "Yes."

"And did you get wet looking at me, imagining what it would

feel like with me over you, against you?"

"Y-yes."

He pulled me closer until the heat from his chest caressed my nipples. Oh, he was going to kill me with his sexiness. His thumb drifted over the artery in the side of my neck. A simple touch, yet I gasped, feeling another deep zing in my belly.

He bent forward until his warm breath bathed my lips. I held still, desperate for him to kiss me again. He held my gaze for a long moment, then his lips touched mine.

Pure magic. Pulsing heat. From a mere brush of his lips. His scent filled my senses, making me giddy. I tilted my head even as I molded myself to him, clutching his shoulders.

He took my response as permission to devour me. I was drowning in Colt, and I wouldn't have it any other way.

He kneaded my ass as he plundered my mouth. I whimpered. I needed to pull back, to drag in much-needed air, but I refused to lose our connection.

Colt released my mouth, bent, careful of my injury, and lifted me into his arms. He strode across the short expanse of the living area and into the bedroom we'd scoped out earlier. He settled me on the queen-sized bed and covered me with his body, again careful of my thigh as he settled between my legs. Then, he paused, dragging a deep breath into his lungs. He met my gaze, his eyes smoldering with passion even as concern filtered in.

"You've been through a lot, and I don't want to take advantage of you."

That concern was for me. It made something in my chest ache, like it needed to crack open. "Please kiss me again. *Please*, Colt."

And he did, and it was even better because I could use my hands to explore his back, his tight hips, that firm, fantastic butt. But it needed to be naked—*we* needed to be naked.

He ground his erection against my core with a thoroughness that told me how much he wanted me but with a gentleness that showcased his care.

No one had ever treated me so tenderly before and desire warred with affection even as passion overcame caution. He continued to kiss me, learning my every secret.

After a long session of delicious making out, he scooted off me and put his hands on the bare skin of my stomach where my long T-shirt had ridden up.

"Can I take this off?"

I sat up in a flash, ignoring the pain in my thigh, and removed the shirt. His chuckle drifted over my nerve endings. With a gentle palm against my shoulder, he pushed me back to the bed. His hands slid over my breasts the soft fabric of my bra rubbing against my nipples. He continued, down my ribs and over the curve of my waist to the tops of my jeans and panties.

He slid his index finger under the elastic, and I shuddered.

"What about these?" he asked.

"Take them off. Everything off. I want you," I said. My voice was breathy with need.

"And I'm desperate for you." He mumbled something that sounded a lot like, "Fuck. You're perfect."

He trailed his fingers from my knees up over my hips, and I could only moan at the soft, searing touch.

Colt's eyes sizzled with heat as he removed the last of my

clothing with exquisite care. He settled on his side next to me and removed my bra. His palms covered my breasts and I arched up into him, stilling at the sting in my leg.

"Shh. I've got you, Tawny," he said.

He tweaked my nipple to an even firmer bud before he took it in his mouth and sucked hard. I arched again, an incoherent sound parting my lips. He molded my other breast to his hand before turning his attention there.

My core clenched and warmed under his ministrations. I gasped and quivered and cried out as he worshipped my body.

He kissed his way down my stomach, rimming my navel with his tongue before plunging it into the small opening. My body shook and flushed as pleasure swept over me. He ran a hand over my mound, cupping my sensitive flesh. The heat and the slight roughness in his palm caused my internal muscles to spasm.

When he parted my lips and pressed a finger inside, my entire body tightened. He eased in and out with smooth, measured strokes, and I gasped, struggling to remain still when all I wanted was to roll on top of him and take him deep in my body.

"That's it," he murmured against my ear. "Take your pleasure."

I panted. He bit my ear lobe even as he pressed his thumb against the bundle of nerves outside my entrance, his finger finding more inside my walls.

I bowed, breathless, and then I released, turning to kiss him with desperate hunger. He kissed me with equal passion.

I collapsed back onto the sheets, my breathing choppy.

He settled up on an elbow.

"Please," I said.

"What do you want?" he asked. His eyes were dark and stormy, and his chest heaved with each breath.

"You. Now."

With a smirk, he reached toward the nightstand, but then his smile faded.

"No condoms."

If he hadn't looked so distressed, I might have laughed at the situation. "Are you clean?"

He jerked, his gaze flashing back up to lock onto mine. "I've never had sex without one."

"I have an implant. And I haven't had sex in…" An embarrassingly long time. "More than a year," I said. "I'm clean, but it's your choice." I wrapped my legs around his waist but raised my eyebrows.

His face softened as he looked down at me. "It's been about six months for me."

That was a travesty. I already knew this man rocked my world, so it should be illegal for him to go more than a day without bringing me to orgasm.

Wait. No. That wasn't…I didn't mean…

"If that's okay?"

"What?"

"Did you space out on me?" Colt asked. He smiled but he looked unsure. "If you don't want this…"

I tightened my legs around him, aware this was probably my only chance to have him. "I do. Desperately."

He positioned himself at my entrance, and we both moaned at the contact.

"Ready?" he asked. His voice was tight.

"Yes."

Colt pushed inside me, and I reveled in the thick, heavy slide. Skin on skin. I'd never been with a man who hadn't worn a condom. This was…different.

He pulled out and slid back in even deeper. "So good," he said.

No, it was amazing.

Finding a rhythm, he eased in and out in slow, languid strokes. My body heated with his careful thrusts.

Soon, I was shaking with need. Colt kept a hand behind my injured thigh, stabilizing my leg. So thoughtful. So aware.

Then he began to plunge in earnest. His teeth caught his lower lip as he stared into my eyes.

"So damn good," he moaned.

Together we tumbled over into lush, thick pulses of pleasure. He collapsed onto me, and I held him tighter. Soon, he'd move. Soon, the moment would end.

And all too soon, Colt would leave me.

Chapter 23 | Colt | Monday

As my body's lethargy ebbed, it was replaced by something that felt suspiciously like guilt. My breathing returned to normal, but my heart rate remained elevated.

What the fuck just happened?

Clearly, I knew what had happened—I had sex with Tawny. But that wasn't sex—that was...

I rolled to the side and squeezed my eyes shut. Fear mixed with the guilt as it ripped up my chest, clogging my throat.

Shit. Shit, shit, shit. I'd *connected* with her. No way could I claim that was just a release of tension. Maybe it was the lack of a condom? I'd heard guys talk about the skin to skin experience. Much as I wanted to grasp onto that option, I didn't want to lie to myself.

Tawny made me feel; Tawny made the experience richer, deeper...perfect.

"Are you okay?" she asked, her voice tentative.

I hated that I'd given her a reason to question me or what we'd done. None of this was her fault.

Well, it kind of was her fault because she'd pushed for us to have sex just as much as I'd wanted to love her.

What? *Love?* No. *No.*

Had I learned nothing from my time with Kara? And, sure,

Tawny said she had an implant, but how did I know that, really? What if she'd set this whole thing up, all of it, to try to get her hands on my dad's wealth?

What if she was in league with Kara? What if she was *worse*?

"Yeah." I choked on the word. After a sharp inhalation, I tried again. "I'm good. I should be asking you. How are you feeling? Did I hurt your leg?"

All my willpower went into meeting her eyes. I felt so damn raw, and my gaze dipped to her flushed breasts, the smooth skin of her belly, and the sexy flare of her hips. I wanted her again. Even with these questions swirling through my head…even wondering how far she'd go to snag a wealthy man…I was hard. As if the most intense orgasm of my life hadn't just ripped through me.

I tensed. She must have felt my response because she tensed, too.

Her eyes widened and tears built in them.

"Um, I'm fine. I'll just go to the bathroom, and…"

She fled.

I threw my arm over my eyes and groaned. I let her leave the bed upset. Fuck me, I was a moron.

———

After cleaning up and dressing, I headed out of the bedroom, my steps leaden with the weight of my guilt.

I knocked on the bathroom door, and it creaked open a little. I hesitated, not wanting to disturb her, not wanting to have this conversation.

The water was running. I breathed out a sigh of relief. She must be taking a bath.

Then, I heard the sob.

Every muscle in my body clenched tight. Ah, hell. She'd offered me her body, her trust, and I'd made her cry.

Tawny sat huddled in the tub, water lapping her hips, knees pulled to her chest. Her hands were wound tightly around her legs, almost as if she were trying to pull into an even smaller ball.

My heart sank into the growing pit in my stomach and my throat tightened.

This time, I didn't need to force myself forward. Before I realized what I'd done, I was at the side of the tub, my hand on her flawless back.

She jerked and yelped, water sloshing but staying within the deep basin.

"I'm so sorry, Tawny."

She raised her head. Fierce red-rimmed eyes bored into me.

"Shut up and get out," she ground out past clenched teeth.

I stepped back, uncertain by her change in demeanor. I might have left, as she'd asked, if her face hadn't crumpled. She'd lashed out because of my bad response. Because I'd let my uncertainties pollute the beauty of our time together.

I had to fix this.

I shook my head. She made a strange noise—between a grunt and a sigh—even as she looked away. I decided to take that as acquiescence. I pulled my shirt over my head.

I undid my pants, trying hard not to notice the elegant length of her spine, the inward curve at her waist. Tried. And failed.

I shucked my clothes and stepped into the tub, hissing at the heat as it seeped into my toes.

"That's barely warm."

Her shoulders stiffened, but she continued to stare at the taps.

I settled into the water, trying to ignore the angry tingles from the too chilly temperature on my most sensitive places.

I reached for her, but she remained resolute.

"I'm sorry, Tawny," I said again, with a sigh.

She whipped around to face me, her eyes blazing behind the tears glistening in her eyes. "If you apologize again for making lo...for fucking me, then I'm going to leave. I get that you're sorry it happened."

She swiped at her cheeks with jerky, angry movements, and my chest felt crushed under the weight of the mess I'd managed to create.

"I'm not sorry we made love," I said, using the term she'd started to say but cut off. "And I'd love to fuck you soon. But that wasn't why I was apologizing."

I cupped her cheek, trying to ignore her snarl. And how close my hand was to her teeth.

"I'm sorry I hurt you. That I embarrassed you. That I wasn't enough for you."

The anger drained from her face, replaced by confusion. "W-what?"

"I'm sorry I freaked out." I paused, not because I wanted to give the next words more impact but because I couldn't speak past the emotion clogging my throat. I huffed, which caused the water to slosh.

"That was the most mind-blowing experience of my life," I said, forcing the words out. "I...it scared me. How connected I felt to you. How amazing I felt inside you, a part of you…" I trailed off, unsure how to go on.

She stared at me for a long moment, her eyes darting back and forth between mine, seeking… I wasn't sure what. Truth? Honesty?

"I worried you were like…like Kara." I managed to choke out.

If anything, her features grew sharper and anger flowed into her eyes, causing them to darken.

"I am not your ex-girlfriend," she snapped.

"I know that." I blew out a breath. "I know that here." I tapped my head. "But she messed me up here." I touched two fingers to my chest, over my heart. "I'm not proud of my thoughts. But they're mine, those insecurities built over my lifetime because I've dealt first with girls in high school and later with women who never actually wanted *me*. They wanted the wealth and power my father built. I was just…I was just a means to that end."

Her face relaxed, followed by her shoulders. Her arms eased from their grip around her knees and she slowly, wincing, let her legs slide out against mine.

"I'd never do that, Colt. *Never.*"

She looked so fierce, her words so vehement. I tangled my thigh between hers, hoping she wasn't upset with the growing erection that pressed into the softness of her ass. I couldn't help it—my dick wanted a repeat performance.

So did the rest of me.

And that scared me.

She turned over to face me, her chest pressed tight to mine. As

I stared into her eyes, I realized she felt the same way. Not only was I freaking her out, but she'd been attacked, collapsed on the side of the road. She'd been chased, she'd lost her home, and her belief the world she lived in was safe.

And I'd fucked her and fucked up.

"I'm not sorry we were together. Honestly, I'd like to do that again." I pressed my dick against her belly, emphasizing my point.

She sucked her lower lip into her mouth, still mute, watching. Something shifted in her eyes, and I looked at her, seeing the hope springing there.

"I'm afraid," she whispered.

"Of what?"

"You, hurting me."

I embraced her. "Funny. I'm worried about the same thing."

"Please don't hurt me," she said in a small voice. "I'm... I don't think I could handle it, Colt."

I realized two things in that moment: this woman had a straight line to my heart. The one I'd so recently thought I was unable to give to any woman again, ever. And the water was creeping up toward the top of the tub.

I used my foot to turn off the tap because I didn't want to stop holding her.

"You said before that I came out here as opposed to screwing a bridesmaid, and you're right, I did. I ran away from my feelings because they were big and...and...I don't know what to do with them."

I swallowed. "I want to be in the kind of a relationship Clay has with Abbi—the kind that you know is going to last, because the two of them are so freaking in love, you nearly get diabetes standing next to them."

Tawny blinked, her lips parting. "Ah. Jealousy. I wouldn't have expected that from you, Colt. You seem so level-headed. Such a scientist." She rolled her eyes in an exaggerated way, trying to get me to grin, but this was one of my deepest secrets, and I needed to purge all the poison.

"I *am* envious of what they have together. I thought I had that relationship once, but Kara..."

Tawny laid her small hand on my forearm. She was more daintily made than my sister, Cassidy, which was saying something. Cass was small-boned, like our mother, but she'd also been through chemotherapy. Even after two years, Cass remained small for her age and too light for her height. I worried she'd fade to nothing. But my mother told me Cass was stronger than I gave her credit for.

Based on the firmness of Tawny's grip, so was she.

"That's a tough break," she said. "To lose your love while watching someone close to you find theirs."

I met her gaze. "It hurt. Even though I was—am—happy for Clay. I'm older. I assumed I'd get married first. And I never expected to find a woman I could care about on the side of the road."

I brushed her hair back from her brow. "That's random. Sure, life is made up of random interactions, but you...I never could have expected you. Or that what I feel for you could be so deep."

I sucked in a breath. She waited, eyes wide, lips parted.

"I think what freaks me out the most is that part of me feels like I *know* you. Already, after less than a day, you're someone important to me."

She cupped my cheeks, her gaze searching mine.

"You're important to me, too, Colt. And just as unexpected. So, let's do our best not to hurt each other, okay?"

Chapter 24 | Tawny | Monday

Colt and I returned to the bed and lay entwined, sliding into a restless sleep. Afternoon brought a slight chill, so we dressed in our clothes and the added layers of flannel shirts we found in the closet. They were XXL—perfect. Very baggy, but we were covered completely.

After a short conversation, we decided not to build a fire, though we stared at the empty grate. He brought me a glass of water. I was thankful we'd eaten those sandwiches. Colt pulled a slightly-smashed packet of lunch meat he'd snagged before our last cabin, and we nibbled.

"You were smart to bring this," I said.

He shrugged. "Let's hope we don't get food poisoning since it's been un-refrigerated all afternoon."

I stared down at the meat. "Do you think that's likely?"

"No. The temperature in here is still relatively cool, which makes it harder for bacteria to grow. And we need calories. I'm not surprised this place doesn't have any food in it. I'm guessing it's only used in the summer. I'm just glad there's running water."

I chewed my bite of meat slowly. "We are from very different backgrounds," I mused.

"Is that a bad thing?" he asked.

I shook my head. "I don't think so. It's just…" I smiled at a memory. "When I was twelve, I helped my dad extend his cabin so that he could include a full-sized tub. He loved a good soak. He used to take a bath a few times a week. Said it kept him relaxed and focused."

"Hmm. I built stuff but never with my dad. He was on tour a lot when I was growing up. I did my building in camps." He hesitated. "Your way sounds better."

I shook my head. "It's different. Though, I'm thankful for those memories, especially since that's all I have of him now. And I'm sorry you didn't get as much time with your dad as you wanted. I guess being the famous kid wasn't so great. No wonder you shy from it."

I dropped my gaze to my lap, sadness and worry building in my chest. Colt tipped my head up and pressed a soft kiss to my lips. Like all of our kisses, it heated quickly. He pulled back, both of us breathing heavy.

"I like our method of relaxation and focus," Colt said with a leer.

I giggled. We both went back to staring at the empty grate. I was thankful I'd put on those hiking boots at Colt's cabin that morning as I tapped my toe against the hardwood floor.

Good thing we'd regained our senses. Having sex when we did—not our smartest decision and we were lucky not to get picked off in the bedroom. Just the thought of something happening to Colt made my heart speed up way too fast.

"Do you think it's weird that we dressed again? I mean as soon as…"

He shook his head. "We're in a heightened state of arousal—I mean mental arousal, not sexual."

I smiled as he side-eyed me.

"From what I remember from my neuroscience course, being aroused keeps us closer to the fight or flight response. Us being ready to move is a response to that instinct."

She nodded. "Like a soldier who's always ready for war."

"Yeah. I guess."

Silence descended but it was warm, nice.

"I can't believe we started yesterday strangers," I said a while later, needing to break out of the worries running through my head.

"Yeah, that seems a lifetime ago."

I looked up at him. "Thank you, Colt. For everything. I wouldn't have made it through today without you."

"You would have. But I enjoyed today with you."

Warmth spread through me. I'd been so freaked out this morning, so sure I was going to be hunted. But, this time with Colt, in this cabin, felt like a gift. A smile teased around the corners of my lips.

That ended with the faint ping of his phone. He pulled it out of his hoodie. He showed me the screen. An undisclosed number with the code Nick had told us earlier.

"Get your hard drive if you need it. We're going out the backdoor."

I already had it back inside my shirt.

Colt grunted as he headed toward the closet. He pulled jackets off the hangers and met me at the door on the other side of the kitchen.

I set down my glass and picked up the gun. Colt did the same.

"You warm enough?" Colt asked.

I nodded. We moved toward the back door and exited the cabin, me going first, my gun drawn, safety off, finger resting alongside the barrel, ready. My heart thumped hard.

"Clear," I said after a moment. "Let's get to the trees."

I pushed off on my good leg and we bolted out of the clearing around the house and toward the forest.

We made it past the first incline and onto a narrow animal track that wound slowly north. The moon was half-full, giving off just enough light for us to see a few feet in front of us. I tensed when the faint crunch of gravel reached my ears. We kept moving, putting as much distance between us and the cabin—and the people looking for us—as possible.

"You think it's Hemp?" Colt asked.

He held his weapon stiffly, clearly not at ease with it. I frowned, first at Colt's discomfort and then at the approaching sedan.

"Maybe. But the drivers turned off their headlights."

Colt blew out a breath and my stomach flopped. Was he relieved that he'd be free of me soon?

"You're sure we can trust Nick?" Colt asked.

"Yes." My tone was emphatic. "I have to trust someone." I squared my shoulders and faced Colt. "I trust you, and I trust Nick, and Agent Russo."

He cupped my cheek, urging me closer to the long, warm length of his body. "I'm glad I made your shortlist."

He smiled but his eyes remained shadowed with worry.

"You should be," I teased, hoping to ease the tension rising between us. Much as I hoped Colt wanted me to stay, wanted to see if what we were building was real or based on the strangeness of our situation, I didn't feel right asking.

And he didn't say.

"You think they're here?" a deep voice asked, the words filtering up the mountain to us. I paused to listen.

"Your contact said city-boy doesn't do rustic."

"Only one way to find out," another male voice said.

I chewed on my lips, a terrible habit I'd never been able to break. They must have busted open the front door because the resounding slam into the log wall rippled through the quiet woods.

Colt and I bolted along the path.

Chapter 25 | Colt | Monday

We sprinted for a good half a mile before Tawny's breathing turned broken and I worried about her leg.

"Want to stop?"

"Not yet," she panted.

We pushed on. I assumed we were headed toward the meadow—the one Nick mentioned, but I didn't want to push Tawny to talk when she was clearly struggling with the steep terrain.

After another approximate mile, I touched her arm. "Let's slow down. We can't move too fast in the dark. That's how accidents happen."

While the firearm and hard drive weren't heavy by themselves, after too little sleep, vigorous sex, and little food, I worried she had to be near collapse, mainly because I was. I didn't like the idea of her pushing herself past her limit.

We slowed to a walk, albeit a speedy one.

She cocked her head back, as if listening. "I don't hear them, but that doesn't mean they haven't followed us."

"All we can do is head toward the extraction point," I said.

"Yes." She glanced around. "You sure bears are day predators?"

"I'm sure. I thought you worked for Russo."

"I do." She chewed on her lip, obviously nervous. Her voice remained pitched low and soft. "But if Nick steps in, Russo defers to him."

"Seems like the man has a lot of power."

"Yup. And he got it in a relatively short period of time," she said.

At my questioning look, she said, "He's been doing this just a few years. I never got his back story, but he has to be former alphabet—FBI or CIA, maybe NSA, I don't know which agency. He speaks the lingo too well not to be a former operative."

I didn't know what to say. We kept moving.

"Do you know the way?"

"Yes, it's north. Up."

I nodded.

For the first time in my adult life, I was dependent on another person. I'd assumed that would be humbling, but it wasn't. Tawny didn't make me feel lesser because I didn't have the same level of expertise as she did. In fact, she asked me about my navigational skills, admitting her internal compass was terrible. Lucky for her, I had a very good one that I'd honed as an Eagle Scout. So, we complemented each other. I might be dependent on her, but she needed me as well.

We kept moving, but as the night wore on, exhaustion took hold.

"What's your favorite video game?" I asked, mainly to keep myself awake enough to keep moving.

She blinked at me, her eyes bleary. "Oregon Trail."

I digested that interesting tidbit. "Not one of the new awesome graphics games?"

She shook her head. "My dad had this stupid old computer.

It still used floppy disks, one of those was Oregon Trail. I always died of dysentery."

"So did everyone else," I said with a smile. "Or starvation."

"You played that retro game, too?"

I nodded. "And Jupiter Landing. My dad has this slick room filled with old tech. I loved the Commodore 64."

She laughed softly. "I always wanted to take one of those apart. I bet its RAM is pathetic."

"Sure was," I said. "So were the graphics."

We kept up our conversation, using hushed tones.

I found out that we both enjoyed Oregon white wine and action comedies. She'd understood the minutiae of the mitochondrial DNA, listening raptly when I explained its importance in metabolizing alcohol.

While I geeked out, she'd remained focused and asked follow-up questions worthy of a tenured professor, some of which I couldn't answer as well as I wanted.

Once I trailed off, she walked me through some safeguards she'd installed on her machine in an effort to ensure I understood how difficult it would be for the bad guys to track us.

"I still have my phone," I said, my stomach starting to ache.

"That's okay," she said. "Nick will mask it. The protocols are really next level—the same kind used by the NSA," she said, her face earnest.

"How'd Nick get the protocols, then?"

"I helped design some of it."

I smiled, loving that Tawny was as much of a geek as I was. But I hated that she'd been willing to do something illegal, even though

I understood her desire to help and protect her father. I wanted to probe that further, but it seemed that Tawny didn't know much more than she'd already told me. Which was very little.

We walked a bit farther and pale light began to filter through the trees. I couldn't remember the last time I stayed up all night talking to a woman. Maybe never.

Granted, I'd never been in this situation before either.

"Any idea how far away the meadow is?" I asked.

"We've been skirting it for a while," she murmured. "I didn't want to go in until I was sure we had cover."

So, this was it. We were coming to the end of our time together. The realization made a deep pang resonate through my chest. The idea of leaving Tawny to the people who might well have set up her father—and her—left me hollow.

I wanted to protect her.

I wouldn't be able to. Not against this Nick guy. Nor against a large federal agency.

We continued to walk, our pace slower because of our fatigue. At least, that's what I told myself.

"Do you think Nick's here?" I asked.

"Yes," she said.

She stumbled and I turned toward her. The glint of something metal caught at the corner of my eye, and I reacted on instinct.

I had Tawny flattened against the pine-needle and fern-littered soil. She hissed out a breath, and I worried about her leg.

But then bullets pinged into the trees around us. I wrapped my arms around her chest, hooked my leg over hers, and rolled us deeper into the undergrowth.

Bullets sprayed up loam and bits of detritus around us. Tawny's breathing escalated in pace with my own when more boots thundered toward us from behind—followed by the staccato fire of an automatic rifle.

Chapter 26 | Tawny | Tuesday

The world around us exploded in shouts, the reverberation of fired weapons and the smell of gun powder, bark, dirt, sweat, and blood. People in black tac gear and military-grade weapons surrounded us. Colt and I remained huddled together, both of us too stunned to do more.

At least we knew Nick was here.

The shots ended abruptly, and a tall, athletic man stepped over, crouching down at my side. He pulled an earplug from one ear and eyed me, then Colt.

My ears throbbed and my head felt like it was stuffed with cotton, but thanks to the faint strains of early morning light, I managed to read his lips. "No new injuries?" he asked.

I shook my head.

I tugged on Colt's arm to get him to look at me. *Nick*, I mouthed.

Colt's lips compressed and his eyes darkened as he nodded.

Nick motioned for us to stand up, which we did, rather stiffly. I wanted to clutch Colt's hand, but he was a step too far away—already outside my reach. Tears pricked at the back of my eyes.

The magical bubble we'd managed to create even during this period of danger burst. My time with Colt was over.

Nick shepherded us toward a Humvee. A real, armored one

that the Army would use. He offered us each a bottle of water. A few men and women hurried around us, clearly following some tasks neither Colt nor I was privy to.

"Can you hear now?" Nick asked.

His voice sounded warped, and I worried about the damage to our hearing, but I nodded.

"Good. I need a debrief."

"Wait," Colt said. "I have a few questions."

Nick's brows rose and the faintest hint of amusement drifted over his features. "Just a few, Mr. Rippey?"

"A few pertinent ones."

Nick raised an eyebrow, his face settling into a stiff, implacable mask that caused my stomach to ice.

"Why did you really recruit Tawny?"

Nick's eyes gleamed. "None of your business."

"And her father?"

Nick's features shifted, taking on guilt and pain. "Again, not information I'm going to divulge."

"Did you use my dad as bait?" I asked.

Nick's eyes narrowed. They were steely gray—a color that reminded me of mist. The kind that scary things stepped out of.

"No. He used *himself* as bait, but only after he realized what he'd pulled you into."

Shock rippled through my body, followed closely by revulsion. Then anger and relief. So many emotions that my legs trembled. Nick edged forward but Colt was the one who caught me to his side.

"Why was he in San Francisco? He was a sheriff up here."

Nick inhaled sharply. "True. But my group utilizes a team of operatives across the country. We moved him down to the Bay Area for a specific task. Officially, he was on vacation."

"You recruited him," I said, my tone dull. I felt completely overloaded. I was exhausted. Sure, I'd wanted this information, but I didn't like Nick's answers.

"Why him?"

Nick hesitated. "He volunteered." The finality of the tone told me I wouldn't get more out of him by continuing to question him.

"Did you find out who was driving my car?" I asked, changing the subject.

Nick narrowed his eyes. "We found your car. And blood on the driver's seat as well as dots on the dash, windows, gearbox—"

"Okay, I get it." I pressed a hand to my stomach. "Any idea who…?"

"I have some guesses," Nick said. "And I'm pretty sure I'll find out, when we interrogate the surviving mercenary from this firefight, that the same person seen in your car hired them."

"Who?" I asked, confusion causing my skin to itch.

"Ever heard of Bart Novak?" Nick asked.

Though he didn't move or shift, I felt as if his attention hyper-focused on me—on my response.

I shook my head. "I saw the name when I was digging into Howie—Novar, I mean. But, no, I don't know Bart Novak."

"That guy, his company is related to this case, isn't it?" Colt asked.

I swallowed hard. "It's bigger than a private equity firm forcing a company to sell inferior parts to a small luxury jetliner.

And my dad—whatever he thought he was investigating—he never found it."

Colt's warmth passed through his palm and my jacket, giving me the strength to stand up tall.

"No," Nick said. "He didn't."

"Because it was on the dark web. The places you refused to let me search."

Nick nodded.

"Why?" I asked.

Nick's lips pressed tight, signaling he didn't want to answer.

"Military," I said, my heart thundering as I awaited the fall out for my honesty. "The reason you're involved in this case, now at least, is because those parts were sold to and installed on military aircraft."

Nick turned those sharp, cool eyes on me. "I assumed you'd told him already."

"No, and I wasn't sure until you confirmed it." My stomach rolled. "Oh…oh. I just breached my contract," I said, voice cracking. "But Colt needs to know why we've been targeted."

"He deserves to, yes. And I plan to tell you both more on our ride back to Seattle, so don't worry about the NDA Russo's so keen on. Get in."

My muscles quivered as I complied. Colt settled in next to me, taking my hand, he gave my fingers a gentle squeeze.

"If it helps," Colt said, "I already figured out that this was way bigger than Zephyr Corporate Jets."

My hands continued to shake. Possibilities of extended servitude "contracts" flitted through my head. I just wanted free of the

FBI. I swallowed hard as I admitted my deepest wish: I wanted free of my father. Whether it was his past or his reputation, I wanted to move out from under the specter of my father, and finally, finally stand on my own.

I glanced over at Colt. A scratch marred his cheekbone and dirt smudged his chin and neck. He was the reason I longed for a future. And if I knew anything at all about Agent Russo, Colt would be the first thing taken from me in her bid to get me to provide the information she wanted.

Russo would call it incentive.

I called it cruelty.

But I'd been stupid because Nick Fowler knew Colt meant something to me—and Fowler's ruthlessness made Russo look like a cute puppy.

Nick entered the vehicle's passenger seat and turned to face us. His gaze flitted to our joined hands.

"Let me tell you what we know."

———

"A DLA buy?" Nick sat back against the seat as he considered the information. "When did Shasta Aviation get the Defense Logistics Agency contract?"

"I'm not sure," I said. "I set up a time bomb—a program—that should have implemented last night to shut down Shasta's sales. I also built out a Trojan so when anyone tried to access the back end of the sales database, my program infiltrated through that computer and copied all the data from the servers onto a secure location. But my hard drive might have been compromised. I'll have to hook into the system as soon as possible."

I pursed my lips. "All I know for sure, from my initial search before Howie interrupted me, is that his private equity firm finalized its majority-share purchase of Shasta Aeronautics about nine months before the first failure could be attributed to the parts coming from Shasta."

"Your father was investigating Howie," Nick affirmed. His eyes flicked over to Colt. "And his then-girlfriend—"

"Kara," Colt finished. He sounded like a cat trying to degorge a hairball. "They go back that far? When did your dad die?"

I gripped Colt's hand, anchoring him. "Five years ago."

"Kara Horvath is a person of interest. We weren't sure how involved she was with Howard Novak then, but your identification of her helps create a better picture. And from what Tawny was able to send through in her initial search, we can now pinpoint the parts that failed."

"I thought Shasta made 3-D parts to retrofit some of the previous generation aircraft," I said.

"They do. And they're about to get slammed with a lawsuit that alleges excessive profits in addition to knowingly selling defective parts to the defense logistics agency."

Nick motioned to the laptop I cradled. "That is, if you found anything concrete that we can use to show that Howard Novak and his associates intentionally used subpar materials."

My mouth dried. "I don't know what I've managed to pull yet." I glanced over at Colt. "And I didn't know about the Kara connection until I met up with Colt. Howie tended to keep minimal correspondence, which was why I went through the trap door I created to find the second set of books. I'll need to look deeper into the 3-D printing purchases to see if there are answers there."

Colt shifted his jaw. "Kara's legal last name is Horvath?"

"Yes," Nick said, his cold silver eyes fixed on Colt's. "What name did you know her by?"

"Kara Hobbes. And I'm guessing she's not a twenty-nine-year-old marine biology grad student either."

Nick shook his head. Unsettled, I shifted.

"What do Kara and Howie have to do with my father's death?" I asked.

Nick turned to me. Sympathy seeped into his gaze, making my pulse ratchet. "This isn't the first firm Howie's done this to."

"Obviously," I said.

"We think it's possible one of them killed your father."

Chapter 27 | Colt | Tuesday

Tawny's hand spasmed in mine. *Fuck*. Kara had a lot to pay for. And now, more than ever, I was thankful she'd called off our relationship.

But why did she? And why would she show up at my brother's wedding?

I posed both of those questions to Nick Fowler, who closed off and became tight-lipped.

"Let's get you both back to Seattle and processed."

He turned around to face the windshield, effectively eliminating further conversation.

I must have fallen asleep because the next thing I knew, we made a turn into a large concrete building—a parking garage. I began to sit up but stopped once I realized Tawny's head was against my shoulder, her palm pressed on my thigh.

"Good, you're awake," Nick said. He didn't bother to look back; he met my eyes in the mirror. "If you want to make this situation better for Tawny, I suggest you agree to everything Agent Russo wants. *Everything*."

I narrowed my eyes. "Why would you think I'd want that?" My heart pounded at the implicit threat in those words.

"Don't you care about her?" he asked.

I kept my face impassive, hoping I wasn't giving away my feelings. I mean, I'd known Tawny two days. Two freaking days.

Though, it felt longer. My relationship with her felt deeper—deeper than the one I'd had with Kara even though I'd been with her for over a year. My expression hardened as I thought of my ex. She'd used me, and I definitely wanted to help the FBI figure out why, because I worried about my mother's threat to Kara at the wedding. If Kara killed Tawny's father, a trained officer of the law, my mother didn't stand much of a chance.

I would not let Kara hurt my family. No way.

Whatever crossed over my face seemed to signal to Nick that I was ready to listen. I caught the ghost of regret spread over Nick's face.

"When Shepard died, it seemed smart to bring his daughter in before someone else got to her first."

"And you've watched over her? This entire time?" I asked.

I had to work hard not to tense at my frustration with this man. The driver pulled into a parking spot near a metal door. I assumed it led up to wherever Nick wanted to take me.

"Of course. Like I said, she's good. She was also vulnerable. Whatever you think of me, tucking her into the Bureau kept her alive."

"But she's not been happy. Or even that safe."

A faint smile flickered over Nick's lips, but his eyes stayed hard. That must be his default setting. He talked about helping Tawny, but he only knew how to do that by railroading her and keeping details of her father's life from her. I remembered how Hemp spoke Nick Fowler's name—as if he were a messiah *and* the devil. I braced myself for Nick's response.

"Which is why I want you to cooperate with Russo. We want to neutralize the threat to Tawny and to our aviation industry, both private and military. That way we can make sure your brother and his bride are safe, as are the rest of your family members the next time they choose to fly in one of those jets you all own."

Nick waited, let the implicit threat sink in—that unless I did what he wanted, there was a chance my family could be hurt in the future, thanks to faulty equipment. Yes, Nick Fowler was good at what he did. When trying to prod me through my feelings for Tawny didn't work, he changed tactics. He knew how to press into existing fears and emotions.

"This is an opportunity we won't get again," he said. "We haven't been this close to the people in Shep's case since he died. And you damn well better believe I want to nail the bastards who killed her father."

"Her father." Not "my agent." For some reason, that humanized Nick. He might use the people at his disposal but that didn't mean he didn't care what happened to them.

"I'll do what I can. But I don't understand how Kara's involved."

Nick shook his head. "We don't either. But I can tell you that her name has been linked to Howie's for years."

And yet, she'd spent months with me. In my life, in my bed. I couldn't shake the concerns that built as I wondered why.

I looked down at Tawny. Her lips were slightly parted. Her lashes fanned over her pale cheeks, marred by scratches. Her chin remained stubborn even in sleep.

"Will Kara go after my family?" I asked.

Nick hesitated. "I don't know how involved she is, but I do know that Tawny was a target from the moment her father was made. That's why he brought her in—he hoped having her investigating with him, having her on the team, would protect her. When we looped her into the FBI, I'd hoped that would eliminate the threat, but Howie contacting Tawny seems to have reopened our failed investigation then. The question is whether it was incidental or intentional. And I don't know the answer."

"And being involved didn't protect either of them," I said.

Nick shook his head.

"Could Hemp—Shep's former partner—have killed him?" I asked.

Nick's smile was lethal. "He's our third suspect. And as soon as I find him, I mean to ask him that very question."

Chapter 28 | Colt | Tuesday

I stepped into an uninspired beige conference room already teeming with agents. Agent Russo beelined to me—holding up her badge. She was a tall, lithe woman. I'd guess a runner or yoga enthusiast based her lean legs and the strength of her handshake. She wore her dark hair shorn short in a lightly tousled style that I'd bet made some men think she wasn't a threat. Her eyes, like Nick Fowler's, proved that incorrect.

"I understand you have some details for us, Mr. Rippey?" she asked. Her voice was neutral, average.

I wondered if that was beneficial—like her unassuming hair and narrow build. She motioned a place at the table, and I settled there as she sat across from me. Her neat appearance reminded me I'd been hiking through the wilderness all night. Exhaustion weighed on me. That could benefit Russo's questioning—or hinder my memory. She was aware of this probably more so than I.

"First I want to discuss the terms of my cooperation."

Her eyes narrowed. "What did you have in mind?"

"Nick Fowler said that you want to cut off the head and all appendages to this group so that they cannot continue to operate and sell defective parts."

Her mouth tightened. She didn't wear lipstick, so the faint pink color faded. "That's true."

"And you seem to think Kara's been integral to those schemes."

"Wasn't Nick chatty with you," she said, sarcasm dripping from her words. "What else did he tell you?"

I shrugged. "I didn't know Horvath was her last name."

"We know. She uses an alias."

"And she's not twenty-nine.

Russo shook her head. "Thirty-two."

I grimaced. "And I'm going to bet she targeted me for a reason."

Russo gave me a practiced smile. "Besides the fact that your family has wealth and prestige? That your father likes to fly private jets? Well, you're good looking."

I snorted. "Not really selling it as well as she did."

Russo leaned forward. "Did Nick tell you that your cooperation would help us ensure your brother gets back to the states safely?"

That flutter of panic hit my belly again, exploding outward, but then I remembered that Clay and Abbi could fly commercial—or simply stay in their over-water hut and extend their honeymoon. My brother and his wife would be fine. *Safe*. Nick and Russo used this tactic to freak me out and get me to spill all those dirty secrets the FBI hoped I had learned.

"He mentioned it. Just as he also mentioned you'd been in contact with my parents. I'm assuming they're worried about me."

Her smile widened. "Oh, yes. We have them down the hall."

My fingers twitched but I managed to keep them from clenching. I'd wanted to give Tawny more time to rest, but my need to reassure my parents of my wellbeing pressed hard into my sternum.

I met Russo's eyes. "I'm going to help you, but I also want my lawyer present."

My father had drilled the need for representation into all three of his kids. No way I was letting Russo or anyone else pin Kara's activities on me. I also worried that Russo might try to link me to Howie or to Tawny's troubles. No. Talking without my attorney wasn't smart.

"I want Kara to pay for her crimes," I said.

Russo settled back in her chair, the tightness around her mouth lessening. "Good to know. So do we. And we think those crimes include arson."

I closed my eyes. "She set fire to Tawny's cabin?" I asked.

"With Howard Novak inside."

My stomach twisted harder. "After I see my parents and sister, I'll tell you everything I know. And how Nick and I discussed getting Kara to admit to at least some of her crimes."

Agent Russo stood, her chair making an offensive shriek across the floor. "Let me make sure Tawny's inside and accounted for and then I'll bring your parents in."

"Her leg's injured, Agent Russo," I said. "Because you chose not to tell her just how dangerous this particular case might be."

To my surprise, Agent Russo's shoulders slumped forward. "We'll get it treated."

"She's not one of you," I said.

Agent Russo looked over her shoulder, her gaze clashing with mine. "I'm well aware of that. Just as I know our carrot isn't anywhere near as tasty as it was when she started her contract with us."

"I'd like to see her," I said.

Russo shook her head. "Not going to happen any time soon. You have information about a person of interest we need, Mr. Rippey. And Tawny has a job to do."

"I deserve to know she's okay."

"She'll be fine. But you will not interact with our asset—not as long as Kara Horvath is out there, looking for you." Her face softened. "This is for your protection, and hers."

"You mean to protect your case," I shot back.

Her smile was faint. "Smart guy. I can see why she'd like you."

"But Tawny's a private citizen," I said. Concern and something that felt an awful lot like possessiveness burned through my gut. "You can't dictate—"

"We can. And we will." Agent Russo drew herself upright and gave me a hard stare.

"If I think you're going to contact Tawny, I'll confiscate your phone, which will make it harder for Kara to contact you."

Shit. From Russo's mouth, cooperation sounded bad. Like it was mandatory and probably more dangerous than what Tawny and I just survived in the National Forest, which had left me shaken.

I thought about what those two men had said about me. That I was a city boy. They thought me soft—easy prey.

I straightened my spine and sat forward, not bothering to look at my lawyer, Lew, who had just arrived in the doorway. "I want to see my family. And then I want to see Tawny."

Russo rose and leaned forward on the table, getting her face within inches of mine. Shit. I'd overplayed my hand—and my usefulness. Whatever her attachment was to Tawny, it was personal, based on Russo's unyielding expression

"No. Do not attempt to dictate to me again, do you understand?"

Chapter 29 | Tawny | Tuesday

My mind remained fuzzy and my eyes too dry as I made my way down the hall toward the large bullpen where I normally worked. I tried to ignore Nick Fowler as he escorted me into the space. He left me at my usual desk—I wasn't there often, as I much preferred working from my house or the cabin.

Not that I had a cabin anymore. I tried to blame my sadness about its loss on my exhaustion, but the truth was I'd lost the last physical connection to my father in that fire. He might have owned that shack, but it wasn't filled with his books or photos of us together—not the part I'd seen. And he'd never made mention of it to me, which made it feel…forbidden. Definitely not a place I was welcome.

One of Russo's colleagues waited for me to put down my hard drive before suggesting I headed down to the locker room for a shower. "And we can have your leg examined, too."

"It's fine," I said, though the cut felt hot, itchy.

The big guy whose name I didn't know crossed his arms over his chest. "We both know it's not, so humor me."

Okay, then.

I limped a little as I followed him down the back hallway. I halted a few feet from the elevator when an older couple, trailed by a petite teenager with thick, dark waves similar to Colt's pushed open one of the conference room doors.

"Colt!" the woman exclaimed. "I've been so worried. The FBI called to tell us you were involved with that horrible woman…"

The door swung shut. My shoulders slumped. Great. Colt's mother already hated me. I'd really wanted to make a good impression with her—but it wasn't as though I knew when or even if I'd see Colt again. The idea of not doing so caused the snarl of emotions in my throat to grow and the tears to press harder against my eyelids.

The agent in front of me was at the bank of elevators so I forced myself to move forward—away from Colt and away from the dream I hadn't been able to stop from blossoming during our short time together.

"You did that on purpose," I hissed.

He didn't bother to look contrite. "You gotta know where you fit in the pecking order, Reed. You're only as useful here as the information you provide and the criminals you help catch."

The elevator doors opened, and I slumped into the corner. His message was blunt and received: The Bureau wasn't going to take no for an answer. They wanted me to deliver enough information for them to request warrants and search Howie's and Kara's residences.

During my shower and subsequent first-aid treatment by the colossal agent who clearly didn't like me, I kept getting caught in memories of Colt. I missed his dark eyes that seemed to bore into my soul and his comforting presence. I'd been frightened during our escapes, but I'd also known Colt was with me.

Now, I was back to the cold reality of being a team of one

against the world—and I didn't like it.

Colt had been my savior. I'd never expected to need saving, let alone for a man to do it for me. That seemed so...medieval. But Colt had saved my life at least twice, and I wanted to tie my favor or whatever those damsels called it, to his armor and proclaim my interest in him. Unfortunately, I wasn't sure he felt the same, especially after the way we left things between us. Worries circled through my head.

What if our connection was all one-sided? I couldn't ask him once Nick picked us up—it was too personal a conversation to have with agents around, so, instead, I remained quiet. I was good at that. Anyway, why would the hunky guy who could get any girl want anything to do with me long-term? I was just a computer geek, the girl you asked about questions on the test, not the girl who got the guy in the end.

———

I was taken to a small room with a table and two chairs, and the giant-jerk agent, whose name turned out to be Taylor, questioned me. As time passed, I felt like I was about to be charged with a crime. The heat kicked on but still I shivered, wondering what evidence Howie had carried with him to frame me for his crimes.

Russo came in partway through the questioning.

If Colt hadn't found me that first night, I might well be a person of interest in Howie's death. I shuddered. I never wanted the man dead.

I shouldn't have opened the door to my cabin when he showed up. Everything had unraveled from there. But I couldn't be too upset about the situation because it led me to Colt. At the thought of him, of the tender way he'd held me in the bathtub, and, later, in the bed, warmth filled me, doing more than the tepid coffee I was given ever could.

Agent Russo nodded at me, but she told me that one of the techs had my hard drive and would be checking its last usage to confirm my story.

"We received an email from you, but not the data," she told me.

I pursed my lips, frustration twisting through me. I waited.

Russo came back in a couple of hours later to tell me the tech had my hard drive hooked it into another machine. They'd been able to download my initial discovery, along with the email I'd tried to send to Russo days before.

"So, I guess your story checks out clean. But we still need to nail this one down, Tawny, ASAP."

No one stated that I was under further suspicion of illegal activities, but my lack of freedom chafed.

After a full day of questions and research, I couldn't wait to return to my apartment. An agent tailed me home and I was sure another waited outside my building—maybe one inside as well.

Agent Russo provided me with a new mobile phone that had my same number, thankfully. I still had access to my photos of my father and my contacts. But, sadly, I didn't have Colt's number. I'd never thought to ask for it. Still, my photos of my father were a small kindness, but no doubt Russo did so to ensure she knew my location and maybe even to check in on my messages or calls. Much as I hated that possibility, I understood. I was a wildcard from the beginning. This case—Howie—came at me.

I glanced down at the screen, my stomach aching when I saw

the line of texts from my mom. I hadn't had a chance to contact her, but my guess was she'd heard something. While no longer in the state, she'd remained friendly with many of the people my dad used to work for at the sheriff's department. Someone there would have alerted her to the burned-out cabin.

I wasn't ready to call her back, so I set the phone and the apartment key someone at the bureau had gotten for me on my kitchen counter and ensured my door was locked and bolted behind me before I headed to the bathroom where I stripped out of my clothes. After another long hot shower, I dried off, my shoulders tensing when I heard the knock at my door.

"Tawny?"

Colt.

What was he doing here? Russo said we weren't supposed to communicate. My heart pounded.

I slipped into my robe, my long hair dripping down my back as I made my way through the space and to the door.

I threw open the door—and immediately gaped at the sight in front of me. Hemp had his meaty hand around Colt's neck, the barrel of his pistol pressed to Colt's temple. I gripped the door-frame, trying to reorient myself.

"Well? Aren't you going to let us in?" Hemp asked.

I met Colt's eyes briefly, unsurprised to see the fear in them. I held the door wide, wishing Russo had further invaded my privacy and stationed a man on my floor. As far as I knew, no one was in the building. My place was on the fourth floor, two below the top, which would be the only other viable escape—if I could figure out how to get Colt and me out of this situation.

"What are you doing, Hemp?" I asked.

"Tying up some loose ends. Close the door."

The weight hit my stomach hard. I pushed it most of the way but tried to keep it from latching. Maybe someone would notice. Fear bloomed across my still-damp skin and I shivered.

"Me?" I asked, looking over my shoulder. "I'm a loose end?"

He nodded. His face contorted with contrition. "None of this should have happened. If your dad would have just left that job alone, you'd be safe, and he'd be alive."

He continued to move into the room, so I tugged the door, ensuring it was open. What else could I do?

"Get in here," Hemp called.

I shivered, realizing he was in my bedroom.

My phone beeped.

I headed toward the bedroom, but my phone pinged again. And immediately again. Then, it began to ring.

I paused, unsure what to do. Hemp dragged Colt back out of my room, a snarl curling his lips. He shoved his pistol into its holster and grabbed my phone. It quit ringing.

"Your mother."

I swallowed hard and wrung my hands. "Can I just tell her goodbye?" I blinked out tears—not hard to do since I was terrified. "She wanted me to visit her next month. That's the first time I would have seen her since Dad's funeral."

Hemp cursed low as my phone pinged, then pinged again. He continued to stare at it. When it rang, he tossed it at me. I fumbled, my sweaty hands made holding it challenging.

I pressed the "Accept" button.

"Tawny?"

Agent Russo's voice spilled into my ear. I choked a little.

"H-hi, Mom," I said. "It's so good to hear your voice."

I clutched the phone, heart pounding, waiting. "A breach?" Russo said after a long moment.

"Yes, I'm looking forward to that, too. You have no idea how much I miss you. It'll be just like those old times when Dad worked at the sheriff's department."

I hoped Russo could pick up on what I was saying.

Hemp motioned me to finish.

"Unfortunately, I can't talk more right now. I'm tied up…in the middle of something important."

I faked a laugh, not listening to what Russo said. "Yes, yes, life and death. You know me well."

Hemp took a menacing step toward me. I gulped. "Gotta go, Mom," I squeaked. "Duty calls. Love you."

I shoved the phone into my pocket and held my hands up. "It's done, Hemp. She thought I was working on a case. No one knows you're here. No need to hurt Colt."

He narrowed his eyes. "Show me the phone."

I gulped, wishing he hadn't asked for that because I hadn't turned it off.

Had I said too much? I'd probably said too much. But I needed Russo to know who was in my place and why. I slipped my hand into my pocket and pulled out the phone.

I glanced down at it, mind racing, but it was off. I barely managed to hold back my ragged sigh of relief as I flipped it to face Hemp.

"See? You have the power—you're in charge here."

He continued to scowl. "Let's go. Into the bedroom."

He pulled out his gun once more and pressed it to Colt's head. He jerked Colt's arm and Colt staggered a step behind, free hand landing on the counter. Something gleamed for a moment before he wrapped it in his hand.

My key.

I trailed behind.

"Can I put on some clothes?" I asked.

I had no idea where Russo was or how long it would take to storm my door. Stalling seemed like my best bet.

"I just got out of the shower when I heard you at the door, and I'm cold."

I rubbed my arms, realizing this was true. I'd turned my heat down before I went up to the Peninsula, and the past few days had been chilly.

"No. You like that is perfect. More believable as a lovers' quarrel."

"But Colt and I aren't—"

"Don't try to bullshit me."

Colt's face turned into a cold mask of fury, but he remained surprisingly docile as Hemp shoved him deeper into the room. Or maybe he was just concerned about the weapon once again pressed to his temple.

I sure was.

"Get on the bed," Hemp commanded.

He motioned with his pistol, his gaze on me. I caught Colt's glance, saw how the muscles in his shoulders and face tightened.

He planned to do something—as he had at his cabin.

"No," I squealed, stomping my foot. "No, you're not allowed to be one of the bad guys." I grabbed onto Hemp's wrist, letting the real sobs burst forth.

Apparently, I distracted Hemp enough from Colt because Hemp was caught unaware when Colt dipped his knees and came in under Hemp's arm with an open palm to Hemp's throat. He followed it up with a cross to Hemp's cheek. He repositioned the key into a point in his fist as I darted forward and grabbed Hemp's wrist with the gun. Colt jabbed the key at Hemp's eyes, causing the older man to howl and drop to his knees. I leaned in and bit into the fleshy part of his thumb with all my force, knowing the action would make Hemp's fingers less nimble and give us a better chance to get him to drop the gun. My jaw ached and Hemp tried to throw me off, but Colt continued to work his face over with the key and I bit even harder—clamping until my jaw throbbed.

The pistol clattered to the ground, and I spat his hand from my mouth, diving for it.

I came up to find Hemp with Colt in a headlock. I was a good shot, but these were close quarters, adrenaline poured through me at the same speed as fear, and I worried I'd miss Hemp's main body mass and hit Colt.

I shot anyway.

I missed Colt and only grazed Hemp, but it was enough to get the older man's attention. He roared as he dropped Colt and charged two steps toward me. I fired, once again, my chest aching as it rose and fell, my arms trembling.

A thick gush of red bloomed across Hemp's shoulder and down his chest as he teetered and crashed to the floor.

Chapter 30 | Colt | Tuesday

"Oh, God," Tawny moaned.

She was pale, swaying. I stepped in closer and untied her robe. Tawny continued to whimper as I whipped the tie from the belt loops and dragged Hemp's arms behind him. Working quickly, I tied an intricate knot I'd learned as an Eagle Scout before rolling Hemp onto his back.

The man groaned.

"Why did you kill her father?" I asked, glaring at the ash-en-faced man.

"Didn't." Hemp's chest rattled. I'd hoped we'd been wrong.

From the corner of my eyes, I saw Tawny stuff her fist into her mouth as tears coursed her cheeks.

"Then who did?"

"Must've been her."

"Who?"

Hemp's gaze moved to Tawny's, held. "I didn't believe Karina when she said she wanted to participate."

Tawny's eyes came up to meet mine. "That's who Dad asked me to find when he came to me that night. Karina Anderson."

I'd get the details from her in a moment, but I thought I understood the gist: Tawny's father asked her to do an illegal hack job to find this Karina.

"Why were you there?" Tawny asked. Her voice was raspy and thick.

Hemp's gaze glazed. "Had to make sure he wouldn't use her."

FBI agents rushed into the room, brushing hard into Tawny and shoving me aside. Her robe flared open, but she seemed too stunned to notice. I grabbed the edges, holding them together.

One called for an ambulance while another began to work on Hemp's shoulder wound. She'd hit him on the right side, about at his clavicle from what I could see. I stood, my legs so rubbery and numb I worried I'd collapse. My cheek came to her hair and we clung together, both of us shaking and panting.

Two EMTs rushed into the room and dove onto their knees next to Hemp. They worked together in concert, each assured of his or her role. Another paramedic stood in my doorway, the stretcher behind him.

"Stable," the female tech said.

"Excuse me," the third guy said.

Tawny and I maneuvered to the far side of the bed, up against the wall, out of the way, made harder because I held her robe closed, but it also gave me a reason to be close to her. The emergency workers heaved Hemp onto the stretcher and out the door in a blink. Her knees wobbled. I crossed her robe lapels tight and used my free hand to cinch around her waist, holding her upright and keeping her body covered.

"I shot him," she murmured. "Is he going to die?"

Her voice cracked and her wide eyes searched mine. She then buried her nose into my chest, seeking comfort from my body since I could offer none with my words. I held her tighter.

In that moment, I realized something both grand and ridiculous. My feelings might have been based on my need to protect Tawny originally, but they were more than that.

I was falling in love with Tawny Reed.

And that was probably the stupidest decision I'd ever made.

Chapter 31 | Tawny | Tuesday

"I told you to stay away from each other," Russo snarled.

I jolted away from Colt, but he kept me tight in his arms.

"Considering I was pistol-whipped, abducted, stuffed into a car trunk, and held at gun-point, it's not like I could give a flying fuck what you *said*," Colt said even as he ran a soothing hand down my back.

Russo's fists were clenched, and she opened her mouth, no doubt to rip into Colt, but Nick Fowler glided into the room.

"Anything you want to share, Agent?"

Her fury caused her face to mottle.

Nick's voice turned silkier. "Hemp had an interesting comment on his way to the hospital. About how you were the one to tell him where Shep was that night."

All the blood drained from Russo's face. Her gaze darted to Tawny, then away.

"He lied," she said, her back straight, her gaze firm on Nick's.

"Did he? Hmmm. I guess we'll have to sort that out. Why don't we go chat about that—and why you requested Shep for the investigation in the first place."

Russo's fists shook in her effort to get herself back under control. She nodded once to Fowler and walked from the room, Nick a step behind.

He leaned a shoulder against the door jamb, seemingly at ease with the sprays of blood dotting my walls and bed linens. I shuddered. I wouldn't ever sleep in this room again. In fact, I doubted I'd feel safe enough to enter the space.

"Want to get dressed?" Nick asked me.

I nodded.

"Go for it," Nick said. He turned his attention to Colt. "How bad's the head?"

"Hurts," Colt grunted as he touched a spot near the nape of his neck. He winced.

"Too much for you to do something for me?"

I moseyed toward my dresser, dawdling to hear more of this conversation. Nick moved closer to Colt and spoke in a low tone that didn't carry. I scowled but took the hint, collecting my undergarments and jeans and a long-sleeve thermal.

I headed toward the bathroom and gagged at the dots of red coating my nose and left cheek. I'd shot Hemp—for the second time. If I'd known he'd been involved in killing my father back then, I wouldn't have aimed at his leg the last time. I would have shot him in the torso, as I had today.

Still, I didn't understand why he'd come after Colt and me. But I bet Nick either knew or had a suspicion he wanted to prove. That was, no doubt, the *favor* he wanted from Colt.

I tried to get Colt to tell me what Nick wanted but he pretended not to hear me as Nick took us back to the Bureau's offices again. He pointed me toward my desk.

"I'll get your statement later. Get me what you can on Shasta's connections to Novar Capital."

"What about Colt?" I asked.

"I'll talk to him now, then let him head home."

My stomach iced. "Is that safe? For him?"

"I don't have any reason to hold him here." Nick took in my expression, which probably showed my concern. "We'll keep a guy on him, Tawny. I don't want him hurt either."

"Okay." I blew out a breath and refocused on the task at hand. "Novar?"

"Bart Novak's company."

"You mentioned him before—at the clearing. Who is that guy?"

"Howie's uncle. He lives in San Francisco. Where you, Hemp, and Russo were all together—"

"When my dad died." I sucked in my lips and said, "Was murdered."

"That's right." He seemed to ponder something, probably weighing whether to give me the next nugget of information.

"Russo requested your father's presence."

I stiffened. "And you agreed?"

"Russo felt like your father would be an asset in her investigation because he'd done online sex solicitation with a task force here in the Pacific Northwest. He had the training my other guys didn't. And he performed his role perfectly."

Nick accepted two cups of coffee from Taylor, the same giant of a man who'd interrogated me earlier. He practically tripped over himself in his effort to please Nick, who set one of the cups next to my elbow.

"Until something went wrong," I said. Russo might have more answers. Or Hemp. I'd try to find them—I deserved to know.

175

"I've been searching the transactions between Shasta and Novar Capital Assets," I said. "I created a Trojan—"

"Don't want to hear that," Nick said. "I'm in an FBI office now and we can only look at data from legal sources."

My stomach ached. "You want me to dig further into the dark web history. Something to do with Novar."

"Or Bart Novak, Howie Novak, Kara Horvath, Hemp, your father. I need that connection, Tawny. Hemp might not wake up. But we know it has something to do with a woman."

I nodded.

"What about the Trojan I set up?" I asked.

"We'll weed through that later. After you get me this."

I nodded, feeling sick. For whatever reason, digging into the dark web, searching for my father, scared me. He'd been an undercover agent, and I worried about just how far he'd been willing to go—and how much that would change my perception of him.

"Whatever Tawny needs, she gets. Understand?" Nick asked. His voice was soft but it held enough menace for me to sympathize with Taylor. A little.

"I'll do what I can…" I began.

Nick leaned down, his gaze so intense, I suppressed the urge to back away. "Everything hinges on *that* connection in the Bay Area. That's why your father died—because she was involved."

"She?"

"You know her as Kara. Hemp's goddaughter."

I blinked.

He kept his face smooth as he delivered the next blow. "Kara's real name is Karina Anderson."

I raised my eyebrows. The woman her father wanted to investigate was Hemp's goddaughter.

"Russo told me," he said. "Hemp also said Russo was your father's lover."

That statement caused my lungs to pinch. Russo and I would have words. She'd had an affair with my father that I bet coincided with my parents' divorce. The woman who cost me my family—not just the unit but in my father's life.

And she'd kept that hidden from me for years.

She'd also saved my life today. Because she worried Hemp would expose her secret? Or because she actually cared what happened to Shep Reed…and by extension, his daughter?

I pressed my lips flat. "One time, when Hemp was at my dad's place, he mentioned how he helped Karina get an internship," I said. "At Novar Capital."

Nick raised an eyebrow. "And you know this how? Were you in the room?"

I shook my head. "I was supposed to be watching TV. They were on the porch. But I'd been curious about Hemp." My cheeks flushed. "I had a schoolgirl crush on him. That's why I remember the conversation."

Nick smirked. "Interesting intel-gathering method. See if it overlaps with Howie's time at Novar. He worked for his uncle, Bart Novak, before he moved to Seattle a couple of months after your father's funeral."

I picked up the coffee and sipped to get the foul taste out of my mouth. "Where should I start? On the dark web or in the employee search?"

Nick grunted. "Both. Immediately. And…" He hesitated. "And see if Kara or Karina had a relationship with Bart."

Gross. I set my coffee down, my stomach was queasy. I didn't know the man, but he had to be thirty years older than Kara/Karina at least.

"What's going to happen to Colt? Will he be safe now?" I asked.

Nick's eyes narrowed as he studied me. "I don't like to lose assets. Ever."

His eyes darkened, and I finally realized Nick ached with my father's death.

"So, I plan to ensure both your and Colten Rippey's continued survival. That said, you two have proven more adept at ripping open this investigation. Hell, I wouldn't have thought to look into Hemp and Russo until Colt told me you two wondered about Hemp's proximity to Shep at the time of his death."

"Why not?" I asked.

Nick's flicker of disapproval settled over his face. "Because I messed up. I was out of the state when this went down, Tawny. Your father wasn't the only agent we lost. We're still trying to tease out what happened and why—even all these years later. It is, and I hope it'll always be, my largest failure."

I didn't like my father being part of a failed anything. I wanted his death to mean something. Nick must have seen some emotion flick across my face because he leaned in closer.

"Exactly. We're trying to figure out if there's more to the connection between Howie's private equity firm and Shasta's subpar parts and Novar's connection to my men's death five years ago."

"You don't know?" I asked, shocked.

"There's a lot I don't know," Nick admitted. He sighed, and he looked exhausted. "Too much."

"I better get to work, then," I said.

Nick offered me a faint smile. He turned and glowered at Taylor, causing the hulking agent to deflate further. "When she needs to rest, she sleeps. I mean it. Make sure it happens."

Taylor nodded. "I'll get her a pillow."

"And a blanket," Nick said.

Sifting through the new data Nick requested took hours. The monotony of creating a word search and flipping through pages of propaganda. It was the dark web, after all.

The ideology and discussions annoyed me and reading these pages worsened the guilt I'd heaped on myself. I'd gotten Colt embroiled in this mess.

I clicked open another page, my despondency growing. I wished I knew how Colt was faring. Was he still here? I didn't know.

So far, I wasn't getting anywhere. Fine. I switched tactics and created a search based on photos of Kara along with an older one provided in the file when she went by Karina Anderson. A chatroom popped up. My fingers shook as I read through page after page.

Men bid on her picture and profile.

I gaped at the sums of money.

I printed out the pages. There were too many. *One* would have been too many. But from that single chatroom, I found other women. It was challenging because, officially, the pages had been scrubbed from the site.

I had to use a backdoor to the larger site and then tease my way through hundreds of pages, but I found them.

Seventeen others. All young, barely legal. All auctioned off. All the money laundered through multiple shell corporations that...of course! I needed to follow the money.

I created another algorithm and sent it spinning. I sat back in my chair when it pinged with results, my stomach roiling at the financial data that led back to Bart Novak.

Bart Novak had trafficked in young women. He'd sold their bodies and enriched his company—himself. I couldn't deny the reality: my father posed as one of those men. He was supposed to pick up his winnings the night after he was shot. His girl was Karina Anderson. And it was the third time my dad "purchased" a young woman.

I rose from my chair and barely made it to the bathroom before I vomited up the coffee I'd ingested.

Weak, shaky, I flushed the toilet and made it to the sink to wash my hands.

My father had wanted me to look into Bartholomew Nixon. Good old Bart used his father's first name tied to his mother's maiden name when he set up that shell corporation. Bartholomew Nixon was the biggest pimp in the Bay Area.

He was the reason my father died. He was the reason I'd been forced to help the FBI—the reason Nick kept me off the dark web. But it was there, in black and white: a bounty on my father's head. And another one for me. I was worth over three million dollars to Bart Novak back then. No doubt he would have made much more than that by selling my body.

That bounty was discontinued once my father died.

But that didn't explain why Hemp, my father's partner, would shoot him.

Or how Kara and Howie ended up in Seattle.

I rose and walked down the hall to hand off the information I found.

Nick nodded, looking much less haggard than I felt. He glanced up at me. "Want to get some sleep?" he asked.

I hugged my arms to my chest. I shook my head.

Nick's gaze softened. "Then get back on that Trojan horse."

I smiled as I walked out of Nick's office. I snagged another cup of bitter coffee and settled back into my chair, shoving Taylor's feet off my desk. He snorted, coming awake slowly. Once he realized what happened, he glared at me, but I was already focused on my screen.

Shasta Aeronautics proved a bust no matter how deep I poked into their system. If I hadn't found the shell companies through the dark web, I would have thought Novar was clean, too. Nothing of importance stayed on its servers. That had to be a nightmare for auditors—even as it allowed for creative accounting. I did note that the staggering two-billion-dollar valuation was a major market over-inflation, no doubt related to his sex-trafficking. I printed out the documents for Nick.

My eyes ached, and my shoulders and neck were so tense I was surprised nothing snapped when I turned my head.

I was so tired. Exhaustion was making me miss things.

"I'm taking a break," I told Taylor.

He nodded and rose, motioning me to follow him. He led me to a quiet office on one of the distant hallways. The couch had a blanket and a pillow. I staggered toward it.

Once settled on the makeshift bed, I pulled out my phone and sent Colt a message to the number I'd found earlier. The fact that his number was private caused me to have to dig deeper, and maybe that wasn't the best use of my skills, but I needed to know he was safe.

Are you okay?

He didn't reply.

Well, it *was* four in the morning.

———

I returned to my desk before nine. My head still felt fuzzy and my eyes ached from too little sleep and too much screen time. Nick had asked to me skirt my Trojan horse, so I slipped into yet another portion of the firewall at Zephyr Corporate Jets, looking for any of a series of words and phrases. I hissed when I hit serious pay-dirt. Someone used Howie's name and Cayman accounts to cash out a large sum from the same airplane supplier where I'd first noticed accounting anomalies.

"Bingo!" I shouted. Taylor snorted awake for the second time. I pointed to the account in the Caymans and then to the split-screen where the exact same amount of money was taken from the payroll of the airplane supplier.

"Idiot," Russo said. When had she returned? Why was she there?

She answered that question, which she must have seen in my

eyes. "This is *my* department. Nick might have different, often more efficient investigative techniques, but I'm the one who signs off on warrants and searches."

I tore my gaze away, still too angry with her to be civil. "You don't deserve it—not if you send men out into the field to die."

"You have no idea what you're talking about."

"Hemp sent us to the hunting shack. Since I didn't know about you, I had no clue why my dad would keep that place—and keep it a secret."

Instead of the satisfaction I'd expected when Russo paled, I forced myself to blink back tears.

"That's where you met him when you were in town—at the hunting cabin."

She crossed her arms over her chest as Taylor called a judge for a warrant while I printed out the information they'd need. Agent Russo smiled at me.

"You found our link on Howie."

"Don't forget Kara-Karina," I snapped, annoyed she wanted to change the subject.

Her lids fluttered a little. So, she'd learned Kara had been used and abused. Or maybe she already knew…and hadn't pursued options to free the woman. My stomach heaved at that thought.

"Your father…"

"Unless you're going to tell me he wasn't neck-deep in the filth that you sent him into, I don't want to hear it," I snapped.

Her chin came up and she said, "I loved him."

"Yeah, well, so did my mother. At least now I understand why he was so willing to take on those undercover assignments. Made the cheating so much more convenient and further removed from the two of us."

She shook her head, her eyes narrowing to slits. "You don't know what I lost when he died."

Taylor rumbled and we both glared. He stepped back, hands up.

I pushed my face close to hers. "You have no idea what you *took* from me. But I guess since this is your department that you lied, and probably killed, to get, I have to finish this case. Just know it's not for you—it's for my father."

And even for Kara. After what I'd uncovered, no way she wasn't a victim. My stomach rolled as I considered whether she would have killed my father to keep him from raping her, not knowing he was a law officer posing as a John. He would have helped her if he'd been given the opportunity. Instead, my father died, and it was Russo's fault.

Russo's eyes flared. "I'd never—"

I stood, shoving back from the desk, needing air.

"You might as well have pulled the trigger," I said. "He's still dead. And it's because you wanted to continue your affair. He never needed to be in the Bay Area, and he wouldn't have been if you hadn't requested him."

Chapter 32 | Colt | Wednesday

The request Nick made yesterday continued to ping around in my head. I'd asked him what I needed to do to keep Tawny safe. Originally, he'd told me he'd think on it. Last night, while Tawny got dressed in her bathroom, while he and I stood in the blood-spattered bedroom, he'd suggested I should talk to Kara.

I didn't like it, but I'd agreed.

I went back to my apartment where I showered and called my parents, reassuring them I was fine. I even managed a few restless hours of sleep. The worst part of this scheme was the potential fall-out, the first of which started with my mother.

When she arrived at my place, her fear was a palpable entity and her hug held a hint of desperation.

"You're okay?" she asked, her hands cupping my cheeks.

"Yes."

"You need coffee." She headed into my kitchen and started a pot. She got down mugs and poured us each some creamer.

"Looks like you do, too," I said.

"I couldn't sleep. I'm so freaked out. You have no idea how hard it was not to drive here after your call."

"You could have, Mom. I don't want to worry you."

She flattened her hands on the counter. "You're capable of taking care of yourself, clearly, but that doesn't mean I don't worry.

And I'm proud of you for doing so, but I'd really rather you never get involved in something like this again."

"You and me both."

She grimaced. "Your dad doesn't want me to tell Clay what's going on—says it'll ruin his honeymoon. But what if your brother decides to fly home earlier? Or what if he gets on a plane to tour the islands and it malfunctions?"

"I texted Clay again, let him know that he has to wait until we can get an approved plane to him. Believe me when I tell you that he's not upset about the possibility of extra time on the beach with Abbi."

Mom pursed her lips. "What about you?"

A knock sounded and I headed toward the door, asking her over my shoulder, "What about me?"

I glanced through the peephole and my heart stuttered. Tawny was here. I opened the door.

"You scared me, Colt," my mom said, coming up behind me. "That's twice now." She poked me between the shoulder blades. "This woman you helped has dragged you into something nasty."

I caught a glimpse of Tawny's ashen face as she slowly backed away from my partially opened front door. I darted out and grabbed her wrist, which she tried to pry loose. When that failed, she dragged her heels as I tugged her into my place.

"Mom, this is 'this woman.' Her name is Tawny."

Tawny raised her free hand in a small wave. "Also known as the nasty woman," she said, her voice small and tight.

"I never thought you were nasty," Mom said. "I was talking about his ex-girlfriend. I never liked her."

Tawny raised an eyebrow at me as my mother took her in, noting the haphazard bun and the dark circles under her eyes. She pursed her lips and poured a cup of coffee. Warmth lashed through me when she pushed it toward Tawny. Without saying a word, Mom was letting me know she liked Tawny—enough to give her a chance.

"You look like you need this," Mom said.

Tawny stepped forward with a couple of quick tentative steps. "Thanks. The last few days have been…hard."

"Tawny's quick thinking saved both our lives," I said. "More than once."

Tawny sat the mug back on the counter and closed her eyes, her face ashen.

"How are you?" I asked. "Any updates you can share?"

"I'm fine."

Bullshit, but I left that alone.

"Hemp's in ICU. He hasn't woken since…" Her voice trailed off, her face paling.

Since Tawny shot him.

My mom's expression softened at Tawny's obvious distress. She passed me the other mug and then turned around and got another for herself, which she took her time fixing.

"Why are you here?" Mom asked.

"Because I don't want Colt to go talk to Kara."

Tawny turned to face me, those amber eyes too dark with worry. "That's what Nick asked you to do, right?"

"I don't like that woman," Mom muttered.

"Yes," I said. "And I'm going."

Tawny surprised me by stepping forward and pressing her hand to my chest. "Please don't. I found enough information on Howie and his uncle, Bart Novak. Nick has the connection between Hemp and Kara. He'll make sure Russo has enough to ensure a conviction."

She looked so serious as she met my gaze.

I wanted to take Tawny into my arms. I wanted to soothe her as I had last night, but Nick's words echoed through my head: "The best way to get answers is if *you're* asking them. You have the emotional connection that she may respond to. So if you want to know why Kara targeted your family, you're going to have to be the one asking."

That was part of the reason—the main part, but I also needed to see her cuffed for her crimes. I needed the closure for the most colossal mistake of my life—the one that would ensure my family and Tawny were safe.

"No, this is my task."

"But she's dangerous," Tawny said. "Hemp would have *killed* us to protect her. She was there the night my father—"

My voice hardened as I relived the impotency and rage I'd felt in Tawny's apartment. She'd almost died because I'd been stupid—stupid and unprepared. That wouldn't happen again. "Don't tell me what she did. I'm going to get it straight from her."

I'd wear a recording device to ensure the government law enforcement had her confession. Maybe it wasn't the only way to build an air-tight case, but it was something I could do to protect my family. I'd been worried about my mother's threat at the wedding and how Kara would respond. No, I couldn't let Kara hurt my family. And I wanted to protect Tawny, too.

I reached out, planning to grasp Tawny's arms when her lower lip quivered. She stepped back.

"I *have* to do this, Tawny."

Tawny slipped toward the door. "Thanks for the coffee," she said to my mother. Her smile trembled. She faced me. "Goodbye."

Tawny exited before I processed the finality of her tone. I stared at the smooth slab of wood, trying to understand what just happened.

My mom popped me in the arm. "If that's how you treat the women you like, I'm terribly disappointed in both your father and myself. We did a shit job with you."

"I didn't think she'd take it so negatively," I muttered. I pulled open the door, but, as I'd expected, Tawny was already gone.

I rocked back on my heels, gnawing at my lip.

"Tawny should understand that I need to get Kara to admit her part in this. I need to make sure she gets jail time—that she can't hurt you or Cassidy or…"

"Tawny?" Mom asked. Amusement colored her tone. "And for the record, I don't want you to go either."

"What are you saying?" I snapped, ignoring the second part of her comment.

She studied me for a long moment.

"You're going to do this no matter what anyone says," she said. I waited.

Mom placed her hand to her cheek in what I assumed was a self-soothing gesture.

"Why did you ask me about Tawny?" I asked.

"That your reaction—all that hard, unrelenting will you just dished out—didn't make you seem like the hero you want to be. For her."

"Who says I want to be her hero?"

Mom raised her eyebrows, calling my bluff. My cheeks heated. "I can't love a woman after a few days."

Mom settled into one of my bar chairs. She sipped her coffee. "Your dad married me after three."

I walked over. "I didn't know that."

"I didn't want you to know. It seemed…impulsive. And once I found out your father cheated on me, that first time, I left him."

She stared down into her half-empty mug. "I came back for you boys. And because I found out I was pregnant with Cassidy. But your father and I…we've been rocky for years, Colt."

I swallowed. "So you and Dad are…"

She patted my hand. "I'm so glad Clay found Abbi. And that you found Tawny. She's beautiful and clearly smart."

"And definitely not nasty," I said.

She rolled her eyes. "I was talking about Kara, which you know. And I meant what I said about ruining her."

I stared down into my coffee mug, finally processing what Tawny said. Kara *was there the night Tawny's father died.*

Tawny thought Kara killed her father. She came here, trying to protect me, and I flung her concern back into her face—didn't even listen to her. No wonder Tawny left. I'd acted like an ass.

My mom was still chattering. I focused on her, though I wanted to go after Tawny and tell her I'd heard her—I understood her concern.

"I'm glad your father and I didn't poison you boys against intimacy. I worried about that—especially when you dated Kara."

"Why?"

She raised her cup and finished her coffee. "You never worried about her feelings like you do with Tawny. Even if you *are* oblivious."

She shook her head. She met my gaze, cupped my cheek, and smiled but it felt bittersweet.

"Don't miss out on love because you have preconceived notions about it. Don't discount your feelings. And, if you want to be happy, you sure as hell better remember her feelings matter every bit as much as yours."

Chapter 33 | Colt | Wednesday

Planning my meeting with Kara seemed like tactical overkill, but Nick Fowler and Agent Russo were the experts. I listened to their instructions and made mental notes of where each person on the team would be, including the snipers Russo insisted on deploying.

I was fitted with the wire and a tiny camera that set in the top buttonhole of my dress shirt I'd been instructed to wear by a tech while Nick and Russo went over the game plan again. Once the tech left, Nick, grim-faced, settled back in his chair.

"Just so you know, we believe Kara killed him."

But I still felt compelled to follow through on what I could do to help close this investigation. I wanted Tawny to move on—away from the FBI and the memories of her father's death.

"I know," I said. "I saw Tawny this morning. She said you have enough information to implicate Bart Novak and Howie."

"We do," Nick said.

Russo tossed him an angry look. "But we don't know why Howie and possibly Kara chose to promote subpar aviation parts. We don't know why they defrauded the defense department."

Fowler placed his hands, palms down, on the table. "I'd like Kara to answer that. I'd also like to know, for certain, her role in Shep's murder."

Russo stilled.

"How did Hemp know Howie would be at Tawny's cabin?" I asked.

"We don't know that yet," Nick said. "I asked Russo to have another tech dig into emails and phone records while Tawny was in the dark web."

I stiffened.

"She found what we needed," Nick said. "And she found the reason I didn't want her there. We're taking care of Bart Novak and the bounty on Tawny now."

Bounty—the reason Nick brought her into the FBI. Somehow, his words made the whole situation more real.

"The problem is the group surrounding Howie included ten, maybe twelve associates, plus Kara, so the work is slow."

I threaded my fingers through my hair. "Is it always this painful?"

Nick shook his head. "Typically, we can nail a charge and then get someone to talk. But, so far, even though we know the parts that need replacing, and we've managed to shut down Shasta, Howie ran point on that company. With him dead and Hemp incapacitated, we've hit a wall."

"His uncle?"

"Missing," Nick said.

"What's Russo doing about that?" I asked.

"Besides being pissed at me?"

Nick's lips twitched as he glanced over at the woman. She'd been quiet but I could feel the frustration emanating off her.

"Investigating," she snapped. "We're working through the fire scene and another agent is going over Novak's..." She looked at me. "I mean *your* car as well as the one you spotted Kara in, and a third has Hemp's truck."

I nodded.

"Anything you need?" she asked.

Probably. Definitely. "No."

Nick patted my shoulder, while Russo gave a curt nod to a tech. Nick slid out the door.

"I take it you don't approve of his methods?" I asked.

"He was forced out of the Bureau for aggravated assault. I don't know how he managed to start his consulting firm, but his reputation precedes him." She pursed her lips. "Nick Fowler is ruthless."

I digested that information, letting it swirl around with what he'd told me about Tawny and her father. He brought Tawny into the Bureau, not to his organization. If he'd wanted her working for him, she wouldn't have had a choice, which meant there was something there. Something I didn't know or understand—something that might well vindicate Tawny or throw her back into more years with the Bureau and destroy her chances at love.

With me.

Because that's what I wanted. A chance to see if what we'd begun under duress and fear had the potential to be real—like Clay and Abbi.

Nick said he figured Kara must know Hemp's attack on us failed. I'd confirm that when I showed up at her place—if she didn't know already.

———

My legs wobbled as I walked up to the door of her large Bellevue home. I'd arrived on her block with an escort of FBI agents, who let me drive through her gates alone. I felt…exposed and wished I knew where the agents had dispersed. Maybe Tawny and my mother were right, and I was in over my head.

No. I wanted—needed—to do this.

This must be Howie's home because it wasn't the apartment near campus where we used to hang out. Though, I guess now it was Kara's if they'd really married.

She opened the door, her face wan, her eyes dark and bruised looking. Her hair was lank around her head. I'd never seen Kara without makeup, never realized how straight her hair was before. This was a version of the woman I didn't know and it unnerved me.

"I never wanted this," she began.

I sucked in a breath. "What didn't you want, exactly?"

She tugged at her white slacks. I'd never seen Kara in jeans or sweats. Tawny rocked jeans—even borrowed ones.

I couldn't think about Tawny now.

We stared at each other.

"Are you going to come inside?" she rasped. "Or should I stand here so the FBI can cuff me now?"

"Why do you think the FBI wants to cuff you?"

She spun on her heel and headed deeper into the house. After a moment's pause, I followed.

"What happened, Kara? What are you involved in?" I wondered how Kara knew the FBI was probing her.

Kara's shoulders stiffened but she moved forward until she was settled on her loveseat.

I sat on the couch, nearest to the door, just inside Kara's living

room. She sat, stiff and unresponsive, her knees pressed together in her white trousers. The house was the showpiece Howie
intended it to be, and Kara looked quite at home in the opulent
decor of the cavernous space.

"Want to tell me the truth?" I asked.

She narrowed her eyes into slits and grimaced. "No." She
tossed her hair over her shoulder. "But I do want to know why
you're here with the FBI."

"I'm not. I'm here to get answers from you,» I said. "You owe
me that much. Did you marry him?"

She crossed her arms over her chest and glared. "That's none
of your business."

I unlinked my hands and stood. "Then we're done here."

I made it halfway to the door before Kara's voice caught me.
"Wait."

Fear laced the word.

I looked back over my shoulder. "Why?"

"Because…" Tears pooled in her lashes and splashed down
her cheeks. "I can't go to jail. They'll hurt me." She sucked in a
breath. "I'll be hurt again." Her lower lip trembled.

I bit the inside of my cheek. Nick had told me what Tawny
found but seeing Kara like this made my heart ache. She started
out as a victim, too, however she ended up.

"Not my problem," I said.

"You are such an asshole," she shrieked. "You *said* you loved
me. That you'd take care of me."

"That was before I realized you'd lied to me about everything.
Everything, Kara. You knew exactly who I was long before I knew

you. *I* was a target. The question I have is why. What did you expect to get out of me?"

"Your family," she snapped. "They could introduce me to the right people."

"And those would be?"

She rolled her eyes. "Wealthy people. Powerful men."

"Dating Howie gave you that connection," I said. I needed to be careful about how much I revealed.

"Howie was a means to an end," she said.

I waited. She looked so broken as she stared down at her knotted fingers. "He got me out. Away from…away from Novar."

I shoved my hands in my pockets. "Bart Novak sold your body."

She flinched hard, like I'd hit her. Her head dipped once.

"And you shot a man—the man who was supposed to be your next…" I didn't know the right word for it.

She sucked in a breath.

"Did you know he was working undercover? That he planned to help you?"

"No." Her voice was tiny. "I didn't know that. Not until Hemp found me later."

"So, why did you shoot him?"

"Howie killed the agent, not me. But he did it *for* me. And he told me I had to go, right then, if I wanted out of the city—away from Bart." She paced, her skin flushed. "Bart had incentives. I just wanted out of the nightmare."

"So you went with Howie and he brought you to Seattle, under a new name."

"Yes."

"And you lived with Howie?"

She shook her head. "I didn't want anything to do with him. Hemp helped me. He got me back in school, he gave me money for my apartment."

"Then why did you go back to Howie?"

Her lip trembled. "Because Bart found me." She pressed her lips together. "And I was scared."

A dusty coating clung to my mouth. I wouldn't have gotten her out—she would have pulled me *into* this mess. "So, you went back to Howie because…"

"He fixed it before," she said, her voice soft. "He made Bart, the other men, go away."

"But?"

She settled back onto the couch, all fight gone out of her. "He realized I'd lied to him about Shasta."

"How?"

"I…" Her lip trembled but she straightened her spine. "I set up the parts that were sold to the defense department. I skimmed money off the deal." She raised her gaze to me, her eyes wet, tears streamed down her cheeks. "I wanted to get out. I wanted to start over."

"But Howie realized what you were doing," I said. The pieces of the puzzle snapped into place.

"He told me to get out."

"You're the one who set fire to Tawny's cabin."

She looked away.

"And running us off the road?"

Her glaze slashed back to mine. "You had a woman with you. You...you *replaced* me. After you told me you loved me."

There wasn't anything else I could get out of Kara. My head ached as much as my chest. But she'd also hurt a lot of people.

That was something I'd need to tease out. Now wasn't the time.

Kara faced me, desperation on her face. "I love you, Colt. Help me out of this. I did it so we could be together."

No, she hadn't. But the plea wasn't that different from the one she'd made at Clay's wedding. Kara was screaming for help—and I'd do what I could to make sure she received it.

"I can't help you, Kara."

She lunged at me with a shriek. Her nails curled into claws and her face reminded me of Gollum's when he realized Bilbo stole his ring. Her nails raked the side of my neck, and she slammed into me, harder, fighting like a wild fiend. I managed to flip her over and pin her even as I heard the pounding boots of multiple agents.

I glanced up, breathing hard, as Russo stepped into view.

"I've got her," Russo said.

She sank down onto a knee as she pulled cuffs from the pocket of her dress pants and clicked them around Kara's wrists. I sat back on my heels, dazed by the revelations, by the constancy of violence that had permeated my life this week.

Kara's sobs turned ragged, painful. Russo surprised me by crouching lower and pulling the younger woman into her arms, rocking her back and forth. The glimpse I caught of Russo's face told me that she understood Kara's situation better than I could.

I stood, my legs shaky, and walked out of the house, wondering if I'd actually done the right thing.

Chapter 34 | Tawny | Thursday

I glanced out the window of Nick's office, unsurprised by the drizzle. I scrunched further into the chair, still worried about Colt.

I knew Russo had arrested Kara. I knew that Howie was the one who killed my father. I knew that Russo hated her part in it, but my emotions swung too wildly for me to know if I could forgive her.

"Do you plan to renew your contract with us?" Agent Russo asked into the deepening silence.

I shook my head. "This work is important. But it's not for me."

"In some ways, you are the very antithesis of your father. Even when you're acting stubborn and difficult like him."

Her faint smile stuck with me as she stalked out of the room. My shoulders heaved with relief. I no longer needed to worry about any of this. My time bomb had stopped further aviation part sales as it was supposed to. My Trojan horse hadn't functioned properly, but Russo had the information she needed, thanks to Colt.

I was free from this investigation—from Nick and Russo, and even from the hell of not knowing who killed my father.

"He was FBI?" I whispered.

"No," Nick said from my shoulder.

I rose and spun, my heart pattering hard.

"He worked with the agency sometimes, much like you do—or I do. As a consultant. He was still on the sheriff's payroll."

"But that job…" I frowned. "When you came to get me…"

Nick studied me. "Hemp's awake. I plan to talk to him."

I stiffened. "And you're inviting me?"

He nodded.

I fidgeted for a moment. But there were answers I needed and only Hemp would offer them. I shoved the little voice down, not liking how it told me that Colt chose to connect with Kara for the same reason.

When we arrived at the hospital, I forced my shoulders back and stepped past the agent sitting next to the door and into the room. As Nick promised, Hemp was handcuffed to the bed. His skin was pasty and his eyes sunken.

"Tawny," he rasped.

Nick's warmth behind me gave me the courage to take another step.

"I'm glad you're going to live," I said.

Hemp's lips twisted. "Are you? After what I did to you?"

I laid my damp palms against my jean-clad legs. "Did you know Howie Novak killed my father?"

Hemp closed his eyes as regret pulsed over his craggy features. "No. I thought Kara did it."

"Shep figured out that Bart Novak trafficked girls," Nick said. "That's why he wanted you to look into Kara—how he'd found her."

Hemp nodded. "I figured that out later. He wanted you to prove that Bart funneled that money into his private equity firm, which he then used—"

"To buy companies, force them to sell subpar parts, and bankrupted the companies themselves, often hurting others in the process." I paused. "I've found two others besides Shasta. This goes back decades."

Hemp nodded. "I only got involved to try to get Kara out. She'd become a favorite toy of Bart's. Howie wanted her for himself, but Kara ran from him—from everything related to San Francisco."

"Is that why you killed Bart Novak as he fled from Tawny's cabin?"

I jerked, turning to face Nick, eyes wide.

Hemp closed his eyes. "I killed him because he drew a firearm and shot at me. The fact that he hurt young women and enriched himself off their suffering made it much more satisfying."

"Bart was at my cabin, too? Why?"

"Because he'd been tracking Howie's movements," Nick said. "I thought he was the one to set the fire until Kara confessed to it. And she did so to try and cover up the fact she and Howie were not married—she was working to get marriage documents forged so that she inherited Howie's estate."

"To ensure her future," I murmured.

As awful as Kara had been to Colt, I couldn't imagine going through what she'd been forced to endure, and I couldn't blame her for wanting to protect herself with money and power—anything to ensure she was safe from future sex trafficking or retribution.

At the same time, I couldn't condone that or the embezzling of funds, the intentional sale of defective parts. I wasn't sure if it was better or worse that I could understand her motivation, her need for self-preservation.

We remained silent for a moment, each of us clearly lost in our own thoughts.

"I don't understand how Howie knew to contact me…yes, I do. The dark web." I closed my eyes and tilted my head back. There were many threads to this spider web, but they all led back to Bart Novak.

"He must have found something." Hemp met my gaze. "He thought Bart was stealing from him and that you were helping."

"*That's* why Howie reached out to me." I clenched my hand into a fist, unsurprised to see it shaking. I glanced up at Nick. "I never understood why he sought me out." I gaped at Nick. "You knew this."

Nick's neutral mask held but I thought I saw a hint of regret in his hard gaze. "We suspected."

"And the man you caught back then?" I asked.

"Mid-level. Not high enough in the hierarchy to hand us the ringleader," Hemp said. "Plus, he died in jail before you were able to interrogate him properly." Hemp met Nick's eyes.

"You in on that?" Nick asked. His voice was as smooth as a knife blade but sharper—with more potential violence.

"No. I wanted the trafficking scheme exposed," Hemp said. "One of Bart's guys got to him before you or me."

"Why were you there, outside my place?" I asked.

"I didn't want you involved. I knew what Bart did to Kara. I couldn't believe your dad would put you at risk." He glanced up. "Russo told me where Shepard was. I wanted to save him, Tawny."

His eyes beseeched me.

"I wanted to save Kara. I got her into that mess with Bart Novak." Hemp's eyes filled with tears. "I'm the one who got her that damn internship. I'm the reason Bart sold her body."

Nick took over the questioning then, and I zoned out. Really, none of the rest mattered to me. I shoved my hands into the pockets of my jeans and waited for Nick to finish.

Once he was satisfied, he led me out of the hospital to his large, white SUV. No Humvee in the city, but I'd bet this one was just as reinforced as the Army-grade vehicle had been.

Nick glanced at me as he started the ignition. "You okay?"

I snapped my seat belt into place and stared out of the front windshield, considering his question. "No."

In the next moment, I bawled my eyes out. All the stress and worry seemed to leak out of my eyes and nose.

Nick waited, patient. When I finished he handed me a packet of travel tissues. "Feel better now?" he asked.

I wiped my cheeks and then my nose, using a few of the tissues, which I collected in a soggy mess in my lap. "I'm not sure. I think…I think I need to see my mom."

Nick nodded. "I'll get you a ticket if that's what you want."

I glanced over at him. "You made me work with the FBI to protect me—you knew that case my father was working wasn't tied up."

"Yes."

"Why didn't you tell me?"

He considered that as he drove out of the parking lot. "You remind me of my wife."

My gaze shot to his. His entire face softened. I couldn't see his eyes behind his glasses, but I assumed they shone with the same love that beamed over his face.

"She's stubborn. And she inserted herself into an investigation years ago." His mouth turned down. "She almost died."

"That's got to be a story," I said, my tone light.

He snorted. "Oh, it is. A hell of one—maybe I'll share it with you." He studied me. "I see a lot of Allie in you," he said softly.

I decided that was the best compliment I'd received.

"I think I'd like to meet her. Someday," I said.

His mouth took a rigid line. "She doesn't come near this work. Ever."

I surprised myself by reaching over and patting his hand. "That's okay, neither will I. I never enjoyed it. I want something boring, like correcting potential identity theft breaches."

Nick smiled and his entire face lit up. "Whatever you want, Tawny, I'll make it happen." And he would—Nick Fowler had that power. "I made a promise to your father to keep you safe," he said. He pulled up to a stoplight.

"You did. I don't like how you did it, but I appreciate the end result." I hesitated, but I needed to know. "Are you going to charge Hemp for Bart's death?"

"Not if it was self defense," Nick replied. He raised an eyebrow, a small smile flirting at the edges of his lips. "And something tells me we'll be able to prove it was self-defense."

Of course Nick would. I had no idea how he pulled off these things, but if what I'd heard whispered about around the FBI office was true, then his team managed to "fix" situations like this before—and would again.

"Want me to take you to the airport?" Nick asked.

I thought about my mother's attempts to reach out. I thought of the angry words I'd said to her over the years. I thought about my father's death and this past week where I'd met Colt and lost him to the lure of justice or retribution or whatever it was he needed more than me.

"Yes, please."

Chapter 35 | Colt | Thursday

I didn't expect to see Nick Fowler dropping Tawny off at the airport. I'd driven there to collect Clay and Abbi, who'd flown home early on a commercial flight, much to my parents' relief.

Nick embraced Tawny before placing his hands on her shoulders, looking into her eyes and telling her something. She nodded. I unbuckled my seatbelt and slid out of my car. I needed to talk to her. I needed to make things right with her. A horn sounded as I went to open my door, and I pulled it back just in time to avoid getting it and my leg smashed by a passing bus. By the time I managed to get out, Tawny was gone. Nick caught my eye and dipped his head.

Then, he settled back into his SUV and drove off. I slammed my hands into the roof of my vehicle. Dammit.

Abbi and Clay were walking toward me, faces tanned and sporting wide smiles. Where had Tawny gone? I swallowed down my concern and the driving need to find her, focusing on my brother and his wife. They were home—they were safe.

Because of Tawny. Shit. I had to stop thinking about her. At least for now. I'd figure out where she'd gone. Somehow. Russo owed me a favor. Or maybe Nick…I threw out that idea. No way he'd help me win back the girl I'd let slip away.

My brother embraced me, pulling me out of my head. I

hugged him back, hard, then hugged Abbi.

"I'm so glad you're safe," I said.

"You'll have to tell us about this chick you met and all the craziness," Clay said.

Abbi must have been watching me because she poked him in the side. "When he's ready," she said.

Clay studied me before clearing his throat. "Yeah. Of course. I'm going to put these bags in the trunk."

Abbi slid into the back seat, and I wasn't surprised when Clay hopped in next to her. He clasped her hand and pulled her closer, pressing a kiss to her brow.

"Tell me again how you two met," I said, hoping the topic would get them to stop fucking each other with their eyes.

Clay told the story with Abbi adding a few additional interesting tidbits of information.

"And you got engaged mere months later?" I asked, though I knew the answer.

"Yeah, man," Clay said.

"When you know, you know," Abbi said.

I glanced into my rearview mirror in time to catch the look they exchanged. I was pretty sure that was exactly how I looked at Tawny.

My former hypothesis that love took time might have been just as wrong as my belief that I didn't know what I wanted in a woman. I knew. *Tawny.* She was who I wanted.

———

I spent the rest of the day with my family, but my mind kept drifting to Tawny. I really wanted to hold her. I wanted her by my side, just as Abbi stood next to Clay.

I stared down into my water even as I smiled at something my father said. He and my mother were trying to work their issues out—for each other, but for us, their kids, too. I wondered if I would ever know such selflessness. I grimaced as I thought back to how jealous I'd been of Clay for finding his love when I should have been celebrating his happiness.

"Want to talk about it?" Clay asked as he settled next to me.

I shook my head.

He bumped my shoulder with his. "Maybe you'd feel better. Kind of like I felt better when I finally vomited out my problems to you."

I smiled. "I have an interview."

"Oh?"

"At the University of Wyoming. It wasn't really on my radar until the department contacted me a couple of weeks ago. They're doing some interesting research into cell antibodies."

"Sounds...intriguing."

I laughed. "You'd hate it, but it's what I love." I sighed, once again staring down into my drink.

"Then why don't you seem happier?" Clay asked.

I met his gaze. "I miss her. A lot. And that feels silly. We don't really know each other."

Clay contemplated me for a long moment. "I knew Abbi's character within twenty minutes of talking to her in the library. I knew she intrigued me when I chased her down. I knew she scared me during our first date."

"I get what you're saying. Mom said something similar. But

things didn't work out great for her and Dad."

Clay rested his forearms on the countertop next to me. "I love Dad, but he can be a selfish prick," Clay said.

I side-eyed him but didn't comment.

"And he's nowhere near as strong as Mom is. *Mom* is the reason Cassidy's alive. *Mom's* the reason Dad still has us to come home to. She could have made her life easier and dumped his cheating ass. But she didn't."

"For us," I said. "I'm not sure that's right for her."

Clay shrugged. "It might not be, and I'll support her if she changes her mind. But I do know that Dad's better with her. He's stronger, more grounded. If he's smart, he won't forget that ever again." Clay tipped his cup back and crunched on some ice.

"Abbi's strong, too," Clay continued. "She had those horrible pictures, those guys claiming all kinds of crap, and she stood up to the bullies—got in their faces and put them in their place. You know, I wonder if we're ever as strong as the women in our lives."

He slid away before I could answer but I didn't have a ready one, so I kept leaning against the counter.

All at once, it hit me: I was scared. Like my father, like Clay had been. I'd finally met a woman I cared about so much I'd willingly risked my life to save hers. And I let her walk away.

I was a damn idiot.

Chapter 36 | Colt | Friday

The next morning, I headed into the FBI office and asked for Agent Russo. She met me in the drab conference room that I'd sat in the first time I entered this building. That seemed like ages ago, not less than a week.

Agent Russo strode into the room and glared at me. "I do work, you know."

"I know. I just hoped you'd tell me where Tawny went."

"All I can tell you is that she's no longer a contractor with the FBI, which is a shame. She was one of our best."

"I need to find her," I said.

"Why?"

I swallowed down the lump in my throat. "Because I think I hurt her feelings, and that's bothering me. Because I miss her company." I forced myself to keep meeting Russo's eyes. "Because I care about her and want to tell her that."

"I don't know where she is, and I couldn't tell you if I did. That's a breach of…something." She shrugged as if what didn't really matter. She wasn't going to tell me.

"Fowler allowed Tawny to leave Seattle. Her contract is fulfilled with the financial records she exposed."

"I don't get why she had to work for you," I said.

"She didn't have to—she was encouraged."

I crossed my arms. Russo sighed. "We were trying to protect her. If she'd delved into the sex trafficking ring further, she might have been killed. Novak had already put a target on her because of her connection to Shep."

"And you never mentioned that to her?"

Russo looked defeated. "The girl just lost her father. She was scared she was going to lose her degree, her licensure…yeah, we took advantage of that, but it was to see if we could draw Novak out. Instead, he went deeper underground. If Howie hadn't reached out, we might never have been able to connect all these pieces together."

"Why didn't you just ask her?"

Russo looked away. "I didn't deem that the best choice."

"But using her was?" Annoyance caused my voice to turn sharp and I wondered if she could feel the serrated edge of my anger.

"You can dislike my choices—"

"I do—"

"But they kept her safe. Alive. And, now, she's solved not just the sex trafficking case but the aviation one. DOD is relieved. She's a hero."

I thrust out my jaw, disliking the narrative Russo set forth. I wondered how Tawny handled being around the woman for so long. She was ambitious, sure, but she was more ruthless than Nick had been. That revelation surprised me.

Of the two of them, I'd rather have Nick nearby. Huh. Still, I hoped it didn't come to me ever needing either of them to save my ass again. Dealing with them once was more than enough.

Russo seemed to come to the same conclusion. "Just so

you know, and so you don't call and bother me again, Kara's being formally charged with embezzlement, thanks to Tawny's findings, but I have a feeling we'll go soft on her because of the extenuating circumstances."

I frowned. "Did you need me to talk to Kara at all?"

Agent Russo chuckled. "Nope. That was for you more than us, though you did get her to spill more details about her past than we'd known. Now, she's being very cooperative, especially if it means dismantling that prostitution ring."

My shoulders slumped. Tawny had asked me not to see Kara, out of concern for my wellbeing, and I blew off her feelings.

"Don't you have a job interview to set up in Laramie?" Russo asked.

Surprise at her question had me studying her again. "Yeah."

Russo pursed her lips. "That might be exactly where you want to go."

This time, I raised an eyebrow. Tawny had mentioned her mother moved to Wyoming after the divorce. She'd also said she wanted to patch up that relationship.

"Are you match-making, Agent Russo?"

She snorted and walked out of the room.

Chapter 37 | Colt | Sunday

I shivered and pulled my beanie low over my ears as the Wyoming wind slammed into my thick coat.

As I turned toward the restaurant the concierge suggested, I caught sight of the woman I'd come to find. No, I wasn't as good with computers as Tawny, but I knew how to search for divorce records to find Tawny's mother's name, and I then applied her name to a search in Wyoming. Luckily for me, Julia Reed still went by her married name and she worked as a social worker in Laramie.

I'd planned to drop by Mrs. Reed's house later, but this was better. I hoped.

Tawny was walking down the street in front of a woman with a small boy and a teenaged girl. Her long, dark blonde hair shone in the setting sun, giving her a halo not unlike a painting of an angel. But she wasn't an angel—she was a warrior. Fierce and unrelenting.

I loved that about her.

Her being there, just as I was thinking of her, *had* to be a sign.

From the moment I'd scooped her up from the side of the road, Tawny meant something to me. Her unwillingness to quit drove me to do better.

Just like Clay said. But, really, it was Tawny who taught me to act on it.

I strode across the street and right up to her. A beatific smile broke over her face as I shoved my fingers into her hair and planted my lips over hers, refusing to wait another minute for her to know just how much I wanted and missed her.

She hummed in the back of her throat, her fingertips brushing my stubbled jaw before sliding into the hair on my nape beneath my black beanie.

I pulled back as both our hats started to tilt from our heads. We parted, only inches separating our lips, our chests, as we struggled to catch our breath.

"Damn, I've missed you," I murmured.

"I've missed you, Colt. So much."

I smiled even as I bent my head to kiss her again.

This time, I tangled my tongue with hers, needing as much of a connection as I could get. She pulled away, breathless, cheeks pink, with an embarrassed laugh, as something small slammed into her leg. Her bad one. She teetered for a moment, arm going around the small body in a thick red puffer coat, while I rearranged her in my arms.

"This is Danny," she said, beaming at me as she ran a hand over the woolen cap pulled over the boy's ears.

"You shouldn't just kiss girls," Danny shouted. "You need to ask them first."

I nodded, my expression solemn. "You're right. I'll do better."

"If you're kissing Tawny, you can't kiss other girls," he said, his scowl fierce.

I leaned in so that we were eye-to-eye. "I don't want to kiss other girls."

"Okay, then," Danny said, grinning, showing off the gap

where his two top front teeth should have been.

"My mom's been teaching them about consent." Tawny turned, one hand sliding down to slip into mine while she kept the other on Danny's shoulder. "She's fostering these two right now."

I nodded, filing away that information.

"Where's Mom and your sister?" Tawny asked.

Danny pointed, and an older version of Tawny waved, her smile a bit sheepish as she approached.

"Sorry for the Danny attack. He was too excited to wait for you to...ah...finish."

"Mom, this is Colten Rippey. Colt, this is my mother, Julia. And that lovely young lady is Alina."

"Pleasure to meet you," I said, holding out my hand. I stepped next to Tawny. I wanted to slip my arm around her waist, but I felt less sure, thanks to her chaperones.

Julia studied me even as she held out her hand. "She said you were a sexy Clark Kent, and she was so very right."

Alina made a choked sound, clearly horrified by her mother's comments. Tawny looked uncomfortable and Danny zoomed around us all, making car sounds, much like any typical young boy. He seemed to be about seven. This crew would fit right in with my family, I decided. In fact, next Christmas, I hoped to have them all at my parents' big house near Bellevue, doing just this.

"We were on our way to the diner to grab some dinner," Julia continued. "Would you care to join us?"

"If you don't mind me joining, then dinner's on me," I said.

Chapter 38 | Tawny | Sunday

My concerns that Colt and I no longer had any chemistry faded as soon as his lips touched mine. We *definitely* had chemistry. And now I yearned to act on it. But I also wanted to know why Colt was here—and what it meant for his, for *our,* future.

We crossed the black-and-white checkered linoleum and settled in a booth toward the back of the restaurant. Alina talked about her plans to eat breakfast for dinner while Danny chattered on about getting extra fries.

I touched my lips, shocked to learn that my desire for Colt was still a firebolt in my belly. No, it hadn't been the danger of the situation that caused our passion; it was us—and the pulsing heat between my thighs proved my desire was just as strong now as it had been when we were dodging and hiding from bad guys. I'd learned that my breath caught at the sight of him and I wanted, desperately, for the chance to make him mine.

We ordered and ate, Mom and I dancing around each other while Mom also managed to learn more about Colt—a topic I found equally fascinating. I hadn't known what to expect when I arrived in town yesterday, but my mother had been welcoming, and Alina and Danny had been excited to meet me tonight.

It had taken me two days to screw up my courage to reach out to my mother. This dinner was another step toward forging a bond. Much as I needed to continue to rebuild my relationship with my mother—we still had a lot to hash out between us—I needed Colt, alone, in bed and naked, more. *Much* more.

I chewed on my lip, wondering how to extricate myself from this situation. My mom, being awesome, managed it for me. She leaned in and placed a kiss on my cheek.

"He's a good one. Thank you for introducing him to me."

"Mom—"

"We'll talk more. Maybe tomorrow…" She grinned at my blush. "You can come to the house to hang out with Alina, Danny, and Ross."

"Who's Ross?" I asked.

Her smile was filled with love and tinted with concern. "My… well, I guess my partner."

I placed my hand over my mother's.

"Is Ross a cop?" I asked, sobering.

"Nope. An accountant. His lack of risk makes him much more attractive," she said with another smile. She collected her coat, then gathered up the kids' winter gear. "You'll meet him tomorrow for dinner. Don't get out of bed until you have to."

"Gross," Alina groaned again.

Mom and I laughed. Colt turned toward us, breaking off his conversation about the coolest Transformer, a confused expression on his face even as he smiled.

Colt placed my hand that my mother just stopped patting on his thigh.

"You seem happy," he said.

I held his dark gaze for a long moment. "I am. You make

me happy."

His smile bloomed brighter, and I barely remembered to wave goodbye to my mom and foster siblings, so caught up in his radiance.

"See you tomorrow," Mom chirped.

Then, she was gone.

"Let's get out of here," I said.

Colt's lids drooped a little and his gaze smoldered. Then, he gripped my hand and we were out the door.

———

We barely made it back to Colt's hotel room. Well, it was much bigger than mine—more like a suite.

My nerve endings screamed with the need for release even as they begged for his touch. One of his arms slid against the back of my thighs, lifting me up, while the other went to work on my top. It disappeared even as I wrapped my legs around him, adjusting until his erection pressed against the juncture of my jeans.

I wound my arms around his neck, fingers in his hair at the nape, cradling his head as he dropped sweet, soft kisses on my chest, working up to my jaw.

I moaned as he nipped at the sensitive spot just below my ear.

"Don't ever stop making those sounds, Tawny. I love hearing you."

His voice was smoke and musk and pure sex.

I tugged him closer, shoving my chest tighter to his body, making inarticulate sounds of need. He obliged by dipping his head to suck my nipple into his mouth, wetting the filmy fabric of my bra.

We passed into the bedroom and he lowered me to the bed. I kept my legs wrapped tight around him as I rubbed our centers together. We both groaned at the friction, needing more.

I unwrapped my arms from his neck with difficulty—I loved running my hands through his hair—and plucked at the buttons of his dress shirt. When I managed to undo them—I kept getting distracted by his attention to my breasts—I shoved the material off his shoulders. He pulled back enough to whip the shirt off, then he tugged his undershirt over his head in a one-arm, behind-the-head action that made me hotter.

His chest was firm, a freaking Michelangelo sculpture of muscles that caused my core to clench in the most delicious of ways.

I leaned up and returned the favor, laving his flat, pebbled nipple with my tongue.

"Tawny," he gasped. "What you do to me."

He flicked open my bra and spread the material from my chest, rough palms molding my breasts. Those noises I didn't know I had in me grew louder, more demanding.

"Fuck, I love how much you want me."

He slid his hands down my ribs, over my stomach, and undid the button of my jeans. The zipper's rasp heightened my desire to have him touch me.

His large palm cupped my sex, and I arched into him.

"You're so hot, Tawny."

I had no idea if he meant my body or my core. Didn't care. I wanted him inside me.

I skimmed my hands down his sides, reveling in his rough inhalation before undoing his pants and shoving my palms inside the open waistband. I cupped his taut buttocks through the cotton of his underwear, loving that he trembled at my touch.

"Get naked," I said. "Now."

He pulled back and smirked at me. "I have plans before I can be naked."

Before I could respond to his comment, he'd slid his fingers under my panties and pushed one inside my plumped lower lips.

My hips rose from the mattress, but he rolled to the side and used his free hand to splay over my stomach, pushing me back down onto the bed.

"I need you to come," he murmured.

"On your dick. Not your fingers," I panted.

"On both."

Much as I wanted to argue on general principle—he should let me be in charge of my orgasm—he added a second finger inside me and pressed into my g-spot. I gasped as my vision tunneled and I swore stars burst in front of me. I wanted to raise my hips but couldn't. I could only splay my thighs wider and take what he gave me.

"That's it, sweetheart. I want that pleasure. I want you screaming with it."

Sweet tension built in my lower belly, tightening my thighs, hips, butt, and abdominal muscles. He slid his fingers in and out of me, faster, pressing a little harder against that internal bundle of nerves. My thighs trembled. My head thrashed around. I needed to lift my hips.

I orgasmed, hard.

Colt covered my lips with his as the breathless scream ripped from my throat. A pulse of pleasure kicked through my muscles, again, then again, until I was sated.

"That was…"

"A start," he said, his expression nearly harsh with need as he pulled his fingers from me and worked my panties down my legs.

Chapter 39 | Colt | Sunday

I admired her nude body, still flushed with the orgasm I'd given her. Her heavy-lidded eyes met mine and her lips parted just a little.

I shoved my jeans and underwear over my thighs and down my legs, my gaze dragging down to her pretty pink lower lips.

I couldn't wait to slide into her. She'd be tight and warm, a perfect fit.

No way I'd ever forget how good Tawny felt wrapped around me. I gave my dick a firm squeeze at the base, trying to tamp down my excitement.

"You are the most beautiful woman I've ever seen," I said, awed that she was here, with me. That she wanted to be mine.

She shifted a little, giving me an even better view. Her hands came up, cupping her breasts, pressing those beautiful globes together and making my mouth water at the sight.

Whatever she was going to say was lost in the kiss I laid on her as I stretched out next to her once more.

But Tawny wasn't letting me run the show any longer. She raised one leg, wrapped it around my hip, and flipped us so that she was on top of me, her thighs on either side of my hips, the heat from her lips settling over my aching dick.

"Condom?" she asked.

I gestured toward my jeans, relieved she'd asked even as I was disappointed not to feel her bare as I had before.

We were naked, together, so I shoved down my fear and told her so. She hesitated for a moment.

"I…I don't want you to think I'd ever trap you with a pregnancy," she said. "I want us to build something for us."

I kissed her, lingering on her lips, but the passion rose again, consuming us. I pulled back and brushed her hair from her cheek.

"I know you want me for me. And I can't tell you how much that matters."

She trailed her fingertips down my chest before she rose long enough to collect the packet, which I took from her and rolled on. She climbed back onto my lap.

"My turn," she said as she sank down, letting me fill her up in one smooth, thick glide.

I gritted my teeth, her name falling from my lips as each sensation slammed into my overloaded brain.

"You…*so good.*"

"Mmm." She rose up until none of me remained inside her. Before I could protest, she brought herself back down, enveloping me again. My lids slammed shut, and I lost the ability to speak.

I clenched my hands, muscles aching with the need to grab her and set the pace.

She continued the languid, brutal teasing until my balls tightened and my release seemed imminent. I grasped her hips and flipped her onto her back, panting with need.

She stared up at me, eyes wide, but a faint smile graced those sweet lips. I hovered over her as I kissed her, my tongue dancing across hers and delving deep into the recesses over her mouth. I kissed her and kissed her until she arched up, her fingers in my hair, tugging at it, demanding more. Only when she seemed as out-of-control as I was did I slip back inside her.

We broke the kiss, needing air. My heart throbbed in my chest. My balls ached. And still I waited, needing to draw this moment out.

"Colt. I need you," she said as she rested her cheek against mine.

I pulled out, then pumped back in. My pace was hard, brutal even. She took it and matched it. My hips snapped, finding a rhythm that had us both breathless.

The headboard slammed against the wall with a loud thump and I kept going. She made those breathy sounds that drove me mad and I kept up my pace.

"I'm...I'm coming," she cried out.

As her walls convulsed around me, the tingles in my balls and my lower back exploded into ecstasy. My hips bumped hers as I spilled myself deep in her body. Once more I pulled out and pushed in, the orgasm still clawing through me.

I collapsed onto her and immediately shifted to the side, cognizant of my much larger, heavier frame.

"I think my legs are jelly. But, damn, was it worth the loss of muscle control," she said as she turned her head.

I pulled her closer to me as I took in her sleepy yet bright eyes, emotion glowing in their depths.

And I kissed her, so very thankful she was mine.

Chapter 40 | Colt | Monday

I woke to Tawny's gaze locked on my face.

"Good morning," I murmured. I tucked her hair behind her ear.

"What are we doing, Colt?" she asked. She inhaled through her quivering nostrils. "What *are* we?"

I settled against the pillows and pulled her to me. She settled herself on my chest, gaze intent on mine.

"I know we still need to learn more about each other. Like, do you let dishes sit in the sink and get a new towel each time you shower? But I know the important things. I know your character. I know your fearlessness. I know your sense of justice. I know your love for your family. I know you're loyal."

I took a deep breath. "Even though it's only been days, I'm sure. I'm falling in love with you so hard. And I will love you more with each new facet I uncover."

Tears shone in her eyes, making the amber brighter. "I...I love you, too, Colt."

The sincerity of her words warmed my heart, the love shining from her eyes soothed my soul. "I'd like to give us a chance. A real one."

"Me, too."

She sighed. "Then, I can deal with the rest."

I settled her tighter against me. "How would you feel about Laramie?"

She threw her head back even as she wrapped her arms around my neck, holding me close to her heart. "Depends."

I pressed my lips to hers. "I have an interview for a tenure-track professorship tomorrow at the university."

"Oh, that's so cool!" she exclaimed. "Tell me all about it."

So, we snuggled together, and I did. Her growing smile and glowing eyes made me even more sure about acting so spontaneously where she was concerned.

"And, since you asked," I said. "I put my dishes in the dishwasher when I'm done with them, and I do get a new towel every time I shower—preferably right out of the dryer, and…"

I still needed to introduce her to the rest of my family—and I would, soon. I needed to spend time with Tawny getting to know more of how her mind worked. But I wasn't worried. We were committed, in this relationship forever.

Epilogue | Colt | One year later

As expected, Tawny's now-official brother Danny was the first person awake on Christmas morning. The child vibrated with excitement but managed to remain quiet until after seven, something we all appreciated, especially once he told us he'd awakened at five.

He'd taken to my parents and Cassidy with the same gusto he did everything, and they loved him back with equal enthusiasm, which was how my folks, Cassidy, Clay, Abbi, Tawny, and her family, all bleary-eyed, ended up in a mountain of wrapping paper before eight in the morning.

We were all secretly delighted by the boy's boisterousness even if I grumbled about the early hour and the lack of proper caffeine.

Tawny shot me an annoyed glance and I laid my hand protectively over her small baby bump. That had been a surprise. An exciting one, but still one I was getting used to.

"How's baby?" I asked.

Next week, we'd find out the child's sex. I was hoping for a girl who looked just like her but without the tendency to get herself into high-stakes trouble or make rash decisions. Tawny wanted a boy as long as he had less energy than Danny.

When she told my mother that, Mom laughed until she grabbed her stomach.

"Colt never sat still," she managed to wheeze out. "I had his father put a pool in so I could actually keep him and Clay in one place for more than five minutes."

"We weren't that bad," I said, my cheeks heating.

Mom raised her eyebrow. "Remember the time you climbed the garage roof, planning to jump off?"

"Or the time you wanted to walk the length of the fence?" Dad added. "It's ten-feet high and runs the length of the property," he added for Tawny's family's sake.

He wrapped his arm around Mom's waist and the two of them settled together, more comfortable than I'd seen them in years. Maybe their new therapist was helping. I hoped so. I wanted them to be happy.

"Or the time you decided to skateboard down the driveway and almost got hit by that elderly lady. Scared her so badly I had to bring her in for tea," Mom said.

With each story, Tawny's eyes widened, and her face paled.

"Thank goodness Danny's playing and didn't hear these stories," she whispered. "Can you imagine what he'd do to my poor mother?"

"I think Ross and I could handle it," Julia said with a smile. She clasped her new husband's hand, her wedding band catching the light.

"No way I can have a boy," Tawny said, on the brink of absolute panic. "What did you do to me?"

I tipped her chin up and pressed a soft kiss on her lips before I whispered in her ear, "I knocked you up and married you."

She tried to glare but her lips turned up at the corners. I put both arms around her and snuggled her tighter to my chest. This love-thing was pretty great.

———

I smoothed my hand over her bump again, willing the baby to move so I could feel him or her. I was kind of jealous that Tawny could feel faint flutterings while I couldn't.

"How's baby?"

"Cranky because baby's mama isn't allowed coffee," she said.

"Maybe this will help," I said.

I hoisted a large present into her lap.

I'd asked her to marry me before we found out about the baby, but the move to Laramie, and me getting settled into my new position, plus Tawny building up her freelance business, left us both time-poor and we'd postponed setting a date for the wedding.

She ripped off the paper, sending me a quick glance of askance. I kept my poker face. She opened the box and pulled out a framed photo from our wedding, the first one we'd seen since we'd chosen to combine our trip back to Seattle earlier in the month with an intimate ceremony.

She gasped, eyes wide, as she looked at what was my favorite image of the day. She stood, bathed in a ray of sunlight streaming through the venue's high windows, her eyes glowing bright amber, as she looked up at me.

Her ivory dress had a boatneck and tapered to her waist before gently flaring over her hips to pool in a short train at her feet. Her flowers were bright splashes of color, all native to Olympic National Park where we'd met. And she'd tucked the tiny white valerian flowers into her honey-colored hair.

I had my hand clasped around her free one, my face shining with the love I couldn't contain as I stood mere inches from her, sliding on her wedding band.

"It's beautiful, Colt," she said, tears welling in her eyes. She studied it for another moment, ignoring the growing clamor by our families to see the photo. When she turned it to face them, both my mother and hers clasped their hands, eyes soft with love.

"You two are marvelous together," Julia said, dabbing at her eyes.

"Perfect for one another," my mother said.

As I'd anticipated, Mom and Julia had hit it off. So had Alina and Cassidy, who ignored the boring adult gush-fest and bent over their new tech presents, tuning us out as soon as they opened the boxes.

I used my thumb to wipe away the single tear drifting down Tawny's cheek from the corner of her eye. She turned and pressed a kiss into my palm. Her beauty caught me, as it always did, right in the solar plexus. Picking her up from the side of the road was the best stupid mistake I'd ever made. Or ever would.

And under my hand, I felt the first fluttering of our baby.

"I love you," she said.

"And I love you both," I murmured. I nuzzled in closer, my nose pressed to her neck, feeling the reassuring thrum of her pulse. Tenderness and peace filled my chest. "More than I can ever tell you. Thank you for finding me."

She hugged me tightly in those slender arms. My favorite place in the world. "Thank you for saving me."

"Aw, sunshine, you saved me first and last."

ACKNOWLEDGMENTS

Writing a novel can be a painful process. This one was. Maybe it was the pandemic, maybe it was that these characters never wanted to behave as I wanted them to. Whatever the reason, I struggled, and I couldn't have accomplished this book without my family and their continued support. In today's world, especially, I'm even more thankful for my husband and children.

Sarah, you have to be next. This manuscript was a mess when you received it, but you persevered. I'm not sure how, but I am so deeply grateful you managed because it's turned into something I'm proud of. I hope you are, too.

Charity always, always keeps me on task, and I love her for that. Thank you, Charity!

Kathleen, you've made time for me when I probably didn't deserve it, and you made the novel much better with your "nit-picks." Thank you.

Also, many, many thanks to Chris Barker, my weapons consultant.

Chris, the cover exceeds my expectations. You understood my vision far better than I did, and I cannot thank you enough.

A huge thanks to Suzy Sims for coming up with the title. It's a perfect fit! And I can't wait to meet Rosie, the Aussie shepherd, in Magnetic Medic. I hope you're happy with how this book and that one turn out.

To my beta readers, Kate, Antje, Sandi, and Rachel, you are a keen eye and your feedback was invaluable. Thank you for your time, energy, and cheering for this novel. It means the world to me.

To my awesome PR team at The Next Step PR, you ladies rock! Working with you is pure joy.

And to my readers. Well, clearly, without you, none of this would be possible. The fact that you trust me with your time is the greatest compliment. Thank you so, so much.

ALSO BY ALEXA PADGETT

Deep in the Heart
An Austin After Dark Book One
Two strong, battle-scarred people grapple with how to make a relationship work in the forceful first Austin After Dark contemporary. - *BookLife*

She's mending guitars and her life.
Jenna Olsen isn't sure she'll ever escape her past. Becoming a skilled guitar craftsperson helped with the anxiety, but she dreams of the day when she can trust again. When an up-and-coming country star asks for a custom guitar in an impossible time-frame, Jenna falls for the challenge.

He's focused on music to help forget the war.
Camden Grace's music and fans help him cope with the physical wounds he sustained in Iraq. But he's haunted by his fractured family history. When an angry outburst leaves an expensive guitar shattered, he doesn't expect to find a strong-willed woman whose struggle echoes his own.

Will creating a new instrument turn their romance into a smash hit?
As the instrument and their feelings start to come together, a dangerous would-be flame attempts to sabotage their rela-

tionship. The jealous rival could kill more than their careers if Jenna and Camden can't rise above the rage to heal their hearts forever.

Broken Rose of Texas
An Austin After Dark Book Two

She aches to make her own music...but I burn for the perfect revenge.

I never thought a late-night Scrabble game would blow my world apart. Moving letters. Keeping score. Swapping words and desire with a mystery woman who makes me fantasize of things I have no right thinking.

I can't get involved.

I won't.

Despite the pull of her lush curves and the electric crackle of chemistry between us, I resist. Regan has aroused something far more desirable than revenge, and I can't get sidetracked by my pesky feelings. Not now that my plot to pay back my best friend's heartbreaking betrayal finally snaps into place, and I vowed years ago to see it to the bitter end.

And that means no emotional entanglements. *Even* for her.

Until a vindictive smear campaign aimed at Regan is followed by a bombshell that blows my world apart...and our fragile relationship crumbles.

Unless we both go all in and trust each other, we won't be able to pick up the pieces.

Austin By Morning

An Austin After Dark Book Three

Another sultry New Adult Romance from USA Today Bestseller Author Alexa Padgett.

From the moment I see Kate Grace, I can't wait to find out if what they say about redheads is true... Not only are her wild ringlets entrancing, she's sweet and sassy, with slower, sexier curves than a Texas back road.

Too bad she's also country music star Camden Grace's baby sister. Camden holds my chance at a comeback in his hands, and he doesn't want me—or my bad attitude—anywhere near Kate.

I don't have time for all these thoughts about Kate, anyway. I must focus on my son's future. I failed him once, but I'll do anything to prove how much I love him. *Anything*.

Even if that means giving up my dreams of a music career and another chance to kiss Kate's soft, luscious lips. Ike comes first. I promised, and my word is my vow. I'll *never*, ever break it.

Yes, even if I have to give up a chance to work with the biggest names in the music industry, and even if I have to walk away from the only woman I'll ever love...

Sweet Solace

Book One of the Seattle Sound Series

She Knew Him When

When they first met, Dahlia was far too young—seventeen—and already engaged to the wrong man. Her husband eventually betrayed her trust, but Asher shattered her heart when he wrote a song for her…and then vanished.

He Never Forgot Her

Asher's whiskey-rough voice made him a star, but fame extracted its price. After leaving Dahlia Dorsey behind, he never expects the way he'll feel when he sees her next. His once muse is now a widowed mother and a reclusive writer who's given up on happy endings—in part because of his choice all those years ago.

Betrayal Broke Them Once

Dahlia's career is on the rocks. Asher's family is falling apart. Neither can chase a passing attraction. But the connection between them is too fierce and much too precious to resist. When a moonlit beach and the touch of an old friend revives their decades-old cravings, will they be able to forge a bond stronger than past betrayals and youthful mistakes?

Between Breaths

Book Two of the Seattle Sound Series

2017 Readers' Favorite award winner and The Romance Reviews Top Pick.

Grief brought them together

A hospice center is no place to fall in lust. But Hayden Crewe's world is cracking, and he needs something sweet to distract him. It doesn't matter that he's the backbone of Australia's hottest international rock group—here, watching his estranged mother die, he's more alone than ever. So, when he meets long-

legged, perceptive Briar Moore, he knows how to fill the
hole inside.

Fortune will drag them apart

Briar has just escaped a job and relationship that nearly crushed
her. Crawling out of the wreckage of her previous life, she's done
playing it safe. Sexy, vibrant Hayden is what she wants, and Briar
is going to take him. For as long as she can…

Out of heartbreak comes hope

Briar and Hayden plunge into an affair as the ghosts of their
pasts haunt their every moment. While those few, intense days
changed them forever, a connection this fierce should burn out
as fast as it ignited…

Hold You Close

Book Three of the Seattle Sound Series

Searching for peace

Mila Trask's much-wanted pregnancy ended in a crunch of steel
and pain, leaving her career derailed and her body scarred by
a stalker no one else believes in. And Murphy Etsam, the man
she thought would love her forever, shot into international rock
stardom on the pure fury of the song he wrote when they broke
up. Mila must talk to him one last time if she's to fully let go of
her painful past…

Running from the truth

One glimpse of her in the crowd and Murphy knows a year of
drowning his sorrows in booze, fame, and other women hasn't
erased a molecule of his passion for lovely, maddening Mila. Too

bad Mila's stalker picks that moment to attack.

Too close to doubt

With both their lives in danger, the ex-lovers are forced into hiding, where their proximity compels them to face the trauma and misunderstanding that wrenched them apart—and to battle the chemistry that still urges them together. There's no going back to what they had before. But the future is theirs to claim... if they survive.

Many Sounds Of Silence

Book Four of the Seattle Sound Series

An Awful Night

A night she can't remember produces a brutal set of photos the media and former college "friends" won't let Abbi Dorsey forget. No matter what she does, she can't escape the shame and harassment...or the threat of more degradation to come.

A Great Lie

Green-eyed senior Clay Rippey has a famous father of his own, and he knows the sting of betrayal. From the moment he sees Abbi, he can't stop thinking about her. He's not the relationship type, but he can play one for the press to help protect her from the vicious comments circulating about her...

A Dangerous Hope

There's nothing made up about the desire sizzling between Abbi and Clay. But a bond built on fear and faking it doesn't lead to happy endings...

From The First

Book Five of the Seattle Sound Series

Sudden Impacts

The car that slammed into Evangeline Mercer knocked her life apart. Her body will recover, but when she looks at the orphaned girl from the other car, she's lost in memories of her own awful time in the foster system. Evie won't let little Paige go through that nightmare, and she finds an unlikely ally in Kai Luchia, Paige's newest friend and champion…

Hidden Fears

At 22, Kai is the lead singer in a chart-climbing band. He's got frontman good looks and cash to burn. But fame and fortune don't quiet the demons of his past. Or maybe it's just that shy, sultry Evie has given him something better to desire…

Hurried Hope

When Paige's case comes to a crisis, Kai and Evie have one reckless shot to take her future into their hands: get married, and fast. They'll keep her safe. They'll sate the lust that taunts them. And they'll have each other, without any messy feelings to sort out. Unless racing away from the truth leads to a larger crash…

Striker's Waltz

Book Six of the Seattle Sound Series

Take a chance

Because of her violent ex, Preslee Jennings hasn't felt safe enough to date in six years. When she's shoved into volunteering with

Matteo Cruz, soccer star and international sex symbol, she can't deny her attraction. Teo is driven, patient, kind—and his butt is on seventy-foot billboards. Maybe she can risk trusting again, if only for one night...

Take a breath

Battling an injury that could end his career, Teo has one chance left to chase the victory he's sought since he was twelve. He can't afford to be distracted by a fling. Especially not with pretty, talented Preslee, with her watchful eyes and sudden laugh. He can guess she's been hurt before. But the more he sees her, the harder it is to stay away...

Take it all

The growing need between them can't be ignored. If their relationship goes public, the backlash could cost them everything...

When We Fell Down

Book Seven of the Seattle Sound Series

Love played false

It's just before Christmas, and Ella Dorsey is pregnant, heartbroken, and miserable. Her husband Simon hasn't been home in months. There are photos of him snuggled up to his publicist. And just when she thinks things between them are at their lowest, she's served with divorce papers at work.

Too cold to be true

As his life with Ella disintegrates, Simon's music career finally commands the admiration and cash he's always desired. But his son believes rumors circulating and Ella refuses to see him, thanks to those divorce papers he never intended to send. Ella's annual trip to visit her parents in England couldn't have come at a worse time…

An answer for always

Simon has until Christmas to discover the truth, decide what matters, and win his wife back. But there's more to Ella's life than him. For their love to last, he'll have to learn her heart all over again…

A Moonlit Serenade

Book Eight of the Seattle Sound Series

The sound he can't forget

He fell in love with her voice first. But trying to recruit mysterious girl-next-door music teacher, Ryn Hudson, to work on an album together is proving harder than Jake Etsam imagined. She's prickly, defensive, wounded, and stubborn. And he's in danger of falling in love with the rest of her, too…

The hope she can't deny

Ryn has had her share of heartache, and she's not eager to risk a silly crush on an arrogant, unavailable rock star. Jake's band is one of the hottest acts in the world, and for a woman who's already lost it all, celebrity drama holds no appeal. But the man himself is harder to turn away…

The chance they can't resist

As the holiday season takes over chilly Seattle, Jake and Ryn see that something between them glows warmer than twinkle lights. But even if they can stop their doubts, close their eyes, and believe in magic, the pressures of his fame and her past can't just be wished away…

Moonshine Eyes
A Seattle Sound Series novella

Sometimes, one glimpse is all it takes to fall in love…
Seth didn't come to Barcelona for a girl. All he wants is a genuine connection with a rock star father who took off a decade prior. But when he catches the eye of a stunning girl across *Avenida Diagonal*, his plans for a boring, normal life go straight out the window…

After a family secret sent Ramona's engagement crashing to the ground, she fled Milan in a hurry. Her heartache finds a cure the moment she spots Seth. Soon enough, she feels more alive than she ever had with her fiancé.

Even though Seth makes her happy, Ramona can't help but feel the pull of her family back to Milan. She must ultimately make a choice: retreat to the safety of the life she once knew or take a terrifying leap into love.